String of Pearls

DIANNE JUNE

SILVER FOX INK

You Should Know

This novel is a work of fiction with character names,
places, and incidents created by the author's imagination.
Any resemblance is coincidental to any event, location, or
person either living or dead.

The content in this book may not be
suitable for persons under the age of 18.
Due to strong language and adult situations.

Discretion advised.

Copyright © 2021 by Dianne June.

First printing, 2021
Silver Fox Ink
ISBN-13: 978-1-7370438-4-3
www.diannejune.square.site

To New Beginnings

If you got it, it ain't a question

~H.E.R.

CHAPTER 1

Out West

I t was clear for students like me. I was going to have to fuck someone over, or fuck my way to the top. Who and where had yet to be determined.

A college graduate with zero prospects for a job wasn't how I saw my four years at university ending. As an inexperienced student, I didn't fit the criteria, or have the family connections and status required to secure paid internships or employment. I was left in the wind with student loans and memorable semesters of being young, living wild, and a failure.

Word traveled fast in my family. "Amber went off to college and didn't accomplish shit," they whispered. Those whispers circled back to me by way of my proud, cackling aunts who wasted no time to brag about my cousin's successes at the first family gathering. But as my luck would have it, their gossip led me to a golden opportunity in Malibu with Uncle Jeff, the rare rich one in the family.

Catching wind of my dilemma, he offered to pay me a pretty penny to update the décor of his beach house while he traveled out of the country for the summer. I quietly stomped my feet when I got the call, and agreed to travel out west to the California coast and house sit for him. "I'd love you as my first client for my portfolio," I said.

I didn't hesitate to pack and book a flight to what felt like destiny. Fresh air and crystal blue watered beaches surrounded by the wealthy was exactly what I needed to build my resume in the competitive world of interior design. Also, to escape the confines of living with my mother and her rumor mill sisters.

My plan on this perfect escape was to reinvent myself. Uncle Jeff assisted with my scheme without knowing it. On the day of my arrival, he added my name to the guest list of his Country Club membership. He gave me a tour of the grounds then escorted me to the dining hall to taste what he called the best scallops and alfredo orzo dish in the world.

While scouring for an open table, an acquaintance of Uncle Jeff's called us over. Rich Donovan, a financier golf buddy and neighbor stood as we approached.

"Rich, this is my niece, Amber. She'll be taking care of my house while I'm away."

"Lovely to meet you, Amber. I wish my son Derrick didn't stand me up today. You two would have gotten on well." Rich smiled at me as he shook my hand. I stared into his green eyes, wondering if his son was as handsome as he. "If you two haven't had lunch, there's room for you two at my table."

Uncle Jeff looked down at me and I nodded it was okay. "We'd love to." He accepted.

Rich stepped towards me and pulled out my chair. My ass just touched the seat when Uncle Jeff surprised me with a curveball.

"Rich, if you don't mind, will you and Derrick serve as an emergency contact while I'm away. Just in case Amber needs anything while I'm away?"

"We'd be happy to. I'm sure my son would love to show you around."

I played nice and danced around the notion. "I appreciate the offer, but I'm out here to work and make my uncle proud. If I have any free time, I'll let you know."

As Rich and my uncle discussed stocks, business, and politics, I studied his dewy lips. They resembled those of Dean Kelte, my freshman calculus professor. The moment I arrived at university, boys, men, and partying were my priority. Also, the main reason I probably graduated without any prospects of a job. I skated by for four years, screwing whoever I wanted without a second thought, earning the nickname, *'THE FUN GIRL.'* With a moniker like that, more than the students desired promiscuous nights with me. Enter Dean Kelte and our one on one tutoring sessions with my pussy as his calculator. Oh, how I earned that A.

Dean Kelte sparked my interest in older men. Young boys around my age were cute to look at, but older men heightened my senses. And on my nights with Kelte, my imagination came alive. I was his love slave for a year. He coached me on how to properly perform a blow job, or at least how to give him one—slow and sensual at the start, making sure my tongue wasn't lazy, then suck him off tight jawed when he was close to exerting himself. "Give a man the option to come wherever he pleases," he would say. Most of the time he came in my mouth holding a lock full of my hair. Other times he would say, "Open wide," and I'd sit on my knees and show him my throat so he could grin at me devilishly as his seeds oozed on my tongue and dripped to my breast.

"Amber," my uncle called my name, interrupting my delightful daydream.

"Sorry. I was wondering how a piece like the one on the wall over there would look in your guest room downstairs." I said, lying about the painting behind Rich's head.

"I'm sure you'll make it work. We have to get going to catch my flight now. It's good seeing you Rich. We'll speak soon."

"Enjoy yourself Jeff, and I give you my word. I'll be on call for whatever Amber needs." He handed me his card.

I thanked him with an innocent smile across my lips, but the thoughts running through my head were dead set on making sure he kept that promise.

CHAPTER 2

Clueless

I saw my uncle off and the house was all mine for ten weeks. It was a lonely paradise. Big enough for a family of five, with the decorum of an outdated beach rental property.

Settling in wasn't as cozy as I had imagined. The creaks in the walls, and the wind howling above the skylight in the ceiling above my bed took some getting used to. I tossed for a bit my first night, and sketched my ideas for the layout of the sunroom until sleep took me under just before daybreak.

When I rose in the afternoon, I tagged the pieces of furniture to place in storage, and jotted down my plan of attack to get Uncle Jeff's closet organized. He left enough money for me to throw around, comparable to an entry level salary, so adding a bonus to his project wouldn't dent my purse strings.

I worked nonstop for days, finally taking a break to enjoy the beach when the sun was at its peak. Rich visited my dreams every night since I met him, and I was hoping to see him stroll by, and catch a glimpse of me in my apricot colored bathing suit that blended near invisible against my skin tone.

I tanned on top of the hot sand behind the house,

stretched out across a tacky, bright turquoise beach towel I found in the drawer of my room. I relaxed as the cool, salt-water breeze blew my hair freely, rotating my body in the sun until the timer on my phone reminded me to reapply more sunscreen. When it buzzed, I put off going inside and covered with a white sarong to walk down the stretch for a view of the houses along the waterfront.

Carefully, I counted the homes I passed, collecting multi-colored seashells when the water pushed and receded above my feet.

A group of men and women sat under umbrellas when I reached the fifteenth house. The glares from the women were uninviting. The stares from the men were welcoming.

I stopped in my tracks and pretended to look at my watch for the time, then did a 180 as a voice shouted, "Amber!" The sound of his deep voice aroused me. Quickly, I placed one hand on my shoulder so my arm would cover my hardened nipple, and maneuvered my shoulder bag to cover the other. I turned back around towards the group, and met eyes with Rich, waving for me to come join him.

I smiled and waved, "I was actually heading back to the house. Nice seeing you," I said, backtracking away. My speed increased as I trekked back to the house, yet Rich surprised me, jogging shirtless at my side. From the looks of him, he was a healthy man approaching middle age. Tight medium build with defining lines in his arms and abs. Jogging and barely out of breath. "Why won't you join us?" he asked. "I wanted you to meet my son Derrick."

"Which one is he?" I turned toward his party.

"He's at the bar getting a round for everyone. Come back and have a drink. I'll introduce you to him."

"I would love to, but I can't. I have to get back and sign for a package. Maybe another time." I lied.

"All work and no play. You're too young for that."

Rich was clueless I had no interest in his son. If he had the power to read my mind when he said the word play, he would stop pressing the issue altogether. *I had something I wanted him to play with.* Cleverly I rebounded in our chat, "What if you bring him by the house tonight. I should be free around eight o'clock."

"Sounds good. We'll see you then."

CHAPTER 3

Amber Cometh

I regretted agreeing to meet Derrick when the eight o'clock hour arrived. The restraint I practiced pretending to be impressed by his silver spoon accomplishments, deserved a medal of some sort. My fake laugh alone was worthy of being awarded.

Over idle chit chat accompanied by wine, crackers, and cheese, I entertained The Donovans. I found myself fantasizing how taboo it would be if they both followed me upstairs, and checked the box on my bucket list to participate in a threesome. If I gathered the courage to ask, and they obliged, I would award myself a bonus for doing a father and son.

The fantasy in my head faded away every time Derrick spoke. He looked like a younger version of his dad, but lacked his appeal, distinct voice, and conversational skills. I sensed he was phony, and put on a persona in front of his father. But I saw right through his guarded act.

Rich and I drove the discussion all evening, but he never caught on it was he in whom I was interested. I gave away several signals in the way I smiled and stared at him. Engaged

with him. Asked redundant questions about his business—
All went unnoticed. He continued to brag about Derrick's app
idea in limbo, and insisted we *"young folk"* go out and enjoy
the rest of the evening.

After our wine glasses emptied a bottle of cabernet, I gave
up my pursuit and went for a drive with Derrick. Full on
snore and bore. He took me to a party full of snobs where he
felt superior. Sticking his chest out and commanding attention I wasn't interested in giving him. I offered to call for a car
to take me home, but he insisted he drive me.

The ride home was uncomfortable and quiet. My hand
rested on the door handle when we pulled into the neighborhood. Derrick sighed at my eagerness to escape him, "I didn't
make a good impression on you, did I?"

I pressed my lips and raised my brows. He placed his
hand on my thigh and I tensed. "Don't beat yourself up. If I
can be honest with you, I would have preferred your father's
company tonight. Neither of you picked up on that," I said.

Derrick parked the car in the driveway. I tugged the lever
and he reached over me and pulled the door shut. "My dad?
But he's like...Seriously?" He blinked incessantly in my face.

"Don't take it the wrong way. You are a nice young man.
But you're not my type."

"Why didn't you say this before we left?" Derrick's voice
amplified.

"Because he's been pushing for us to meet, and I didn't
know how to say no without being rude I guess."

Derrick's eyes pierced into mine and the side of his mouth
curved. "There is no way I'm going to lose a girl like you to my
father." He leaned over and kissed my lips gently, then let go.
The hand he placed on my thigh traveled up my skirt, slow
and steady, while he studied my reaction to his advance.

I trembled from his touch and exhaled a deep breath as
excitement flowed within me, undecided if I was going to

throw him a pity fuck, and serve myself from the good deed. He pressed his soft lips against mine again, and slipped his tongue inside my mouth. I engaged for a second or two, then pulled back. Derrick begged, "Invite me in so I can change your mind."

He slipped his finger inside my panties, and I parted my legs to let him flicker my clit, then placed it where he needed to rub to make me cream. Softly he rubbed my g-spot in circles. I quavered in the front seat of his truck, slicking his fingers with my essence. I held my chest as I moaned in tune with the vibration below my hips, pleasured from his finger play.

Vigorously he plucked the way I needed him to, and I came in his hands, holding my breath and still. He opened his mouth and ruined my orgasm, "Come on. Invite me up. I know you're not thinking about my old man now."

CHAPTER 4

The Original

y eyes opened and the stimulation between my thighs declined into descent. I removed his hand and stared in his eyes, considering I was the culprit of the bruised ego hiding behind them. The ego of an immature rich kid who I almost invited upstairs for a nightcap.

I could see the spoiled side of him having spasms as his lips twitched and eyes blinked incessantly. "What gives? You know you don't want me to stop," he said.

I contemplated if I wanted to play with danger, and tell him I was still thinking about his father while he fingered me. Not speaking my truth is what led me into the uncompromising position I was in. "I shouldn't have let you do that," I said.

"But you did. And I know that wet pussy wants me to finish what I started." He licked his lips.

"You have a good night."

I hopped out of his truck and rested better than I had since I arrived. The days after my faux pas I worked diligently with zero distractions, completing the reorganization of

Uncle Jeff's closet, and ordering works of art and sconces for the walls.

As I waited for the orders to pour in, I wandered the nearby towns hoping to score rare accent pieces, and corner shelves from independent shoppes. I loaded a few lucky finds from a mom and pop accessory store into my uncle's truck, then crossed the street to see what hidden gems were in a lamp store going out of business.

The wind chimes above the door dinged when I entered. "Everything's seventy-five percent off!" A voice shouted from behind an oak door.

"Thank you!" I yelled, walking towards the floor lamps against the wall.

I browsed the expensive lamps, reasonably priced with the red sticker sale tag. "Do you need help carrying those to your car?" A man's voice asked. I froze for a second then twirled around.

"How are you?" Rich stood behind me freshly groomed with bits of grey tapered in his goatee.

"Great. How are you?"

"Pretty good. I saw you come in here as I was shopping for a new camera lens next door. I figured I would come say hello, and ask how your evening went with Derrick."

"Well, have you asked him?" I folded my arms.

"I did."

"And?" I failed not to smirk.

"He said I should ask you."

As I stared up at Rich's green eyes, my lips puckered, and my mouth watered inside. "Derrick is a nice boy. He just isn't my type," I said.

"Hate to hear it. I thought you two would hit it off." He shook his head.

"Rich, I'm not like most millennials. You know how young

people today hear a song, and think it's new when it's actually a remake?" I placed my finger in my mouth.

"Yeah."

"Well I recognize it's a sample, and I prefer the original over the remix." I glared deep in his eyes.

"You prefer the original over the remix." He whispered to himself.

"It was good seeing you again," I said, luring him in with an inviting lip lick before I walked away.

The ball shifted to his court, and it was up to him if I would be permitted on his ride. Days went by without word from him. I kept myself busy working from room to room, and decided what colors of paint to cover the walls. I hired painters to coat the walls marine blue and storm cloud grey, and opened the boxes of orders rolling in like a kid opening gifts on Christmas morning.

In need of plants and candles to match the theme of my vision coming to life, I explored upscale shops in Beverly Hills, swiping away on luxurious vases, frames, and hardware. I returned back to '*The Bu*,' overwhelmed with an overflow of boxes waiting for me on the steps.

After unpacking the car and carrying the new deliveries inside, I unboxed wall décor, table accents, and bedding items. As I cleaned the mess, I discovered I overlooked one package. It had no return address, or postage markings, and contained an emerald colored silk slip dress.

I lifted the dress from the box, and a card fell to the floor. It read:

Wear this at 5 a.m., & stand on the balcony.

CHAPTER 5

The Dress

I f curiosity killed the cat, I hoped it killed my cat at 5 a.m. I was overdue for a pounding session, and whoever requested I wear a sexy dress while the sky was still black, was sure to give me the thrashing I needed.

I hit the snooze button when music from the clock radio on the nightstand woke me at 4:30 a.m. I covered my face with the pillow for nine minutes until the snooze expired, and hurried to the bathroom sink to apply depuffing patches under my eyes.

I was a mix of emotions. Sleepy from tossing all night, silly but also turned on following instructions from an unsigned card, and curious who I would find on the balcony.

I slipped the dress over my head, loosely pulled my hair back in a tie, and painted my face lightly with gloss, mascara, and blush. I gave myself a once over in the long mirror hanging behind the bathroom door, took a deep breath, then stepped onto the balcony to meet my suitor.

The sound of two clicks and a flash of light appeared from the boardwalk. The silhouette of Rich stood below me. He stepped into the light from the motion *sensored* post beside the house, and snapped pictures of me smiling in his direction. "Look up," he instructed.

I followed his order and witnessed a moon full and bright. It shone on my center perfectly, highlighting the glow of my bosom, accentuated by the low-cut hem on the dress. I stretched my hands wide against the banister and closed my eyes, listening to the clicks of Rich's camera worship me.

The breeze of the cool night air added to the arousal of my nipples piercing through the silk. "Come," Rich said, gesturing I join him below.

I shrieked coming down the stairs, and grabbed the new throw I bought for the sofa. I wrapped it around me and stepped onto the boardwalk, anxious of where Rich was leading me.

He took me by the hand and walked towards the roaring waves. The scent of fresh saltwater mixed with the night air temporarily burned my nose. I sneezed. "You alright?" Rich asked, placing his hand in the small of my back. I nodded and smiled.

The tone of his voice was different from our previous conversations. This was sexy Rich. Courtship Rich. *Gonna* get fucked Rich.

"You look amazing by the way. I saw that dress on a mannequin in town and thought it would look perfect on you. I love it when I'm right."

"I love you finally caught on to my hints. I didn't wear that flesh colored bikini for myself you know."

"Don't think I haven't thought about that little number every night."

I blushed and lowered my head to the sand. The waves grew stronger the further we walked, blowing the throw off of me. Rich caught it and draped it around my shoulders. "Thank you," I said, hoping he kissed me in that moment.

"We're almost there." He smiled.

"Almost where?"

"There's something I want to show you."

"Okay. Did it have to be so early?"

"5 a.m. is when I begin my day. Most mornings I go for a run out here, but today I skipped my routine so I could show you what I see every morning when the sky is clear."

We passed the end of the cul-de-sac to a secluded area of rocks. By the time we arrived, the sun and the moon were sharing the sky. Rich removed the blanket from my shoulders and lifted me by my waist to the top of the rocks. "Pose for me pretty girl," he said. I raised my shoulders, pouted my lips, and tilted my head to the sky while his camera snapped click after click. "My muse," he said, taking his final snapshot.

He sat next to me, and together we watched the sky change from navy to indigo to sapphire during the blue hour. Finally, he took me by the face and kissed my shivering lips until they were warm.

Specks of water bounced on our feet, while our unlocking lips refused to free themselves. Rich's hands rested against my face, and my arms draped his shoulders. Heat formed between us, forcing us to come up for air. We gazed into each other's eyes, desperately wanting to rub skin right there on the rocks.

I removed the left strap of my dress and enticed Rich to kiss my shoulders. He willingly replied. I leaned back in his embrace, passionately sighing for his lips to taste me on the rocks. His foot slipped as he lowered to oblige me, "It's too dangerous to fuck you out here," he said.

I lifted my dress and placed his hand on my breast. He pinched them as I played with my pussy, groaning when the water splashed my toes. "I have to have you now," he said, removing my hand and sucking my slick from my fingers.

"Your place or mine?" he asked, lifting me from the rocks.

"Whichever is closest," I whispered.

CHAPTER 6

Pollock

The iron vine door closed behind him and I took charge. I embraced the overflowing rush of lust which consumed me, and placed Rich's hand on my pussy. "You're throbbing pretty girl," he said.

I nodded and he grunted at the slickness between my thighs. "It stayed wet for you. Now it's yours for the taking." I whispered.

My words ignited a fire within him already burning. He pressed his fingers hard and upward inside my center. I stiffened and held onto his chest, then purred into his strong shoulders. He controlled my body from his hand. He released his grip and I wilted like an abandoned plant, then pushed his palm against my exterior and returned the pressure. I stiffed straight, then exhaled against his chest. *I knew I sensed a beast in him.*

I pulled his shirt above his head, and licked the pecks on his chest, working my way down his well-kept upper body and solid abdomen. My hands trailed his sculpted biceps while he removed his pants, exposing a shroom formed to perfection. "I must admit, I'm a little intimidated," I said.

I dropped to my knees, salivating at the challenge of fitting him into my mouth. I held him with both hands and parted my lips, marveling at his presentation. Rich lifted my chin, "Not yet darling. Me first," he said, tracing my lips with his finger.

My eyes tautened from his confession. With his fingers still posed on my chin, he pulled me up to face him. A soft kiss brushed my lips as I rolled my palms around his cock, shivering to feel it inside me. He grazed his teeth against my neck, and slid the straps of the dress he bought off my shoulders. As it slid down my body, he tasted my bronzed skin and circled my cognac halo, then placed my erect nipple in his mouth.

I ran my fingers through his frosted tips. My mind skipped the foreplay and imagined how I would wail when he gifted me his cock. His hands palmed my ass and he placed me on the island in the center of his kitchen. I called out to him, but he silenced me, sticking his fingers down my throat. "Be patient," he said. My mouth watered and he retrieved his hand from my mouth and placed it between my legs. Lightly he patted my folds with his wet fingers, and I creamed with every tap, huffing of anticipation.

Rich monitored my reaction, pleased with the way my body responded to him. Abruptly he stopped the patting and massaged my upper inner thigh. My pussy thumped from his rubbing and I placed my finger in my mouth, leaning back on the counter. I was overwhelmed by the sensation of an erotic zone never explored before.

He caught me off guard and sucked the zone he rubbed on my thigh. I jumped and he held me in place, mirroring the same suction on the other side, making me yearn for him. My hands squeezed my nipples as my aching lips contracted for his attention. I took back control and guided his head towards my pussy. He firmly sucked my hole, putting out my fire while simultaneously adding to it, and I cried out for him not to stop.

Rich fucked me with his tongue, sternly extending it deep inside, then swiftly stretched it in and out, in and out, filling me with hunger for a beating. "Now," I pled.

Rich rose from worshipping me. "Don't move," he ordered. I obeyed, splayed wide on the countertop, watching his every move.

He opened the refrigerator behind him and placed a bottle of champagne, and a carton of orange juice on the counter beside me, then grabbed a flute from the cupboard. As I lied still, he returned between my legs and teased me with flicks to my slit with one hand, while rubbing his dick in circles against my sodden flesh. I flinched. I yearned. I waited to feel the pressure of his dick break me open.

The flicks transitioned to long concentrated pats on my clit. I stroked my hands up and down his shaft as he mixed the champagne and juice inside the glass, then took a swig of champagne straight from the bottle. "Mmm," he moaned, dropped to his knees, and licked me strong, deep, and slow from south to north. He paused until my lips twitched and pulsated of ecstasy in his mouth. He lifted and gazed at my cave, "That's it. Beg for me baby," he said. I clung to the edge of the counter and he vigorously licked me once more, flicked my clit with his tongue, nibbled on it gently, then penetrated inside my drenched walls. Hard.

I inhaled a sharp breath and held it, clinging to his shoulders. He shot straight to the back of my canal and held his wide head in position, applying pressure as I squeezed.

Eventually, I breathed and he pulled out completely, slid me off the granite top and turned my back to him. He stuck his fingers in my center once more, then drove his wide dick back inside with the same force. "Yes!" I exclaimed. His left hand circled my clit as I gasped from the thrusting and fucking from behind.

He pulled me close with a fistful of my hair and nipped my lobe with his lips, then kissed the side of my mouth. "You pair well with champagne. See for yourself," he said, placing the bottle to my mouth. I sipped what I could, moaning from the stimulation of his handy work, then he removed the finger rubbing me senseless, and fed it to me, followed with a sip from the flute filled mimosa. "You see how good you taste together?" He laughed villainously. I looked back at him and stole a sloppy kiss, then smirked to myself catching a voyeur in the hallway.

I closed my eyes and reached back, holding the back of Rich's head. I was no longer in control, flailing from his kisses to my shoulder. "More," I said.

He grabbed me by the chin and held my mouth open, then poured the cocktail inside before forcing his fingers between my lips. "I'm going to call you my little Amber Cocktail," he whispered, fucking me harder and faster.

Mumbling obscenities, I sighed of elation and slapped my hand against the counter. Words of affirmation crossed my mind as I suppurated sounds of pain and pleasure. Rich held my shoulders tightly, securing his key inside my lock, and dug me out better than I imagined. Every jab was carefully orchestrated with precision, to make me wallow from his touch. I did more than wallow. I yearned for this man's dick in the past, present and future.

My knees started to unlock and my back turned limp. "Ah!" I yelled from the lost count of orgasms I freed.

Rich shimmied side to side in my love and I buckled. "On your knees!" he ordered. I fell to the floor and opened my mouth to taste his essence. He rubbed his tip across my lips, jerking from his base. I moaned gripping his head between my lips with a salacious, wet, soft suck. Rich hollered and pulled back, grabbed a lock of my hair and guided my neck back. He pollocked a pearl necklace around my neck, then placed his dick back in my mouth. I kissed it delicately.

His thighs flexed and his shoulders jolted in a frenzy until I freed him from my grip. I rose to my feet, weak on cloud nine, smeared in his ivory soil. He held on to me, sucking my face until we landed in a tender lip lock. "Amber Fucking Cocktail," he moaned, catching his breath.

"Rich Daddy Donovan." I replied.

CHAPTER 7

The Voyeur

A stammering laugh escaped my lips once Rich's kisses eased from my cheeks. He placed the glass of mimosa to my lips. I sipped it staring into his eyes. He finished it off then grunted, lightly biting my neck while holding me captive in his arms. I wrapped my arms around his waist and mumbled in his chest, "I'm *gonna* get going."

He moaned in my ear and rocked me side to side, dancing without music. "Let's get cleaned up and I'll walk you home."

"You don't have to." I cleared his residue from my chest and stepped into the dress. "Your day may have started, but I'm going to take a shower and sleep off this workout."

"A workout I hope to do again. But I insist I see you get home. I won't have it any other way." His voice lowered pulling me in close from behind.

The walk was surprisingly pleasant. We shared quiet moments swarmed by a cool breeze and risen sun, and shared smiles while holding hands with barely an inch between us. He kissed me goodbye near the wooden gate a few homes down from my uncle's place, and I tread the rest of the way through the sand and up the boardwalk.

A bottle of water called my name when I entered the kitchen. I leaned against the stove quenching my thirst, disturbed by a knock at the front door. *A package this early?*

I crept to the window. "The fuck," I muttered. Derrick's eyes met mine through the glass. I exhaled deeply and swung the door open, posing with one hand on the panel. "*Whatcha doing here Derrick?*"

He shot passed me without an invitation. "You know why I'm here," he said.

I sipped my water while he paced around the living room area like a kid who couldn't have his way. He was hot under the collar and I knew why, but I held in my grin, careful not to incite another temper tantrum. "So that's you huh." Derrick pointed at me shakily. "I never thought you would act on your word Amber. And don't bullshit me. I know you saw me."

He stopped leaving tracks on the plush carpet and stared at me with his hands barricading his mouth. "Yeah I saw you lurking in the hallway. Peeping from behind the wall. Why were you watching us?"

"I don't know. I couldn't believe my eyes. You—with my dad—it makes no sense. You were supposed to be doing those things with me."

"Derrick, do me a favor. Go home. Light a joint. Do a line. Whatever it is you partake in to relax, and get over it. It's not *that* hard to do. Nothing was ever going to happen between us."

"What about the other night in the car?" His eyes changed from sad to menacing.

"What about it? Nothing happened."

"My fingers say different."

"Are you threatening me?" My brows furrowed.

"No. I'm trying to understand you. What are you after?"

I took a long pause and studied the tension in his neck

and fragility in his voice. My silence agitated him, and I couldn't hold back the urge to antagonize his already disturbed spirit. "Now I see. First you were mad Daddy got the piece of pussy you failed to nail. And now you're worried he'll make me your new mommy. The mommy you wanted to fuck." *Not nice.*

Derrick's face burned with anger. I burst into laughter briefly, then pacified the poor lad. "My God, learn how to take a joke," I said. "I'm not after anything. When I'm done with these renovations I'll be out of your hair. I'm sorry you saw what your father and I were doing this morning. We'll be more careful next time."

"Next time!"

"Yeah. Why does that surprise you? I mean you did see how he was..."

"Okay, enough of this. There won't be a next time. Let the old man down easy, finish up here, and get the fuck out of town Amber."

"Wow. First you threaten me. Now you're running me out of town. What is your deal?"

"I mean it. Don't see my father anymore."

"Or what?"

"Or I will expose you for the tease you are."

"Newsflash. I'm no tease. You saw that this morning. Now get the fuck out of my house."

"Your house? You don't belong around these parts," he said, smugly grinning at me on his way out.

I locked the door upon his exit, took a long hot shower, and slept past noon. Leaving the house for an appointment with the tile and flooring company, I stumbled upon a bouquet of white roses at the door.

Hoping these put a smile on your face.
Like the one I haven't been able to erase since you left.
Call me.
~R.

I DID SMILE. I also worried how to get his son off my back. Derrick wasn't fooling me. He didn't want me to get out of town. He wanted me to give him what his daddy got, and prove he could outperform my seasoned lover. But he knew after watching his papa handle me, he would forever be the lost dog in that fight.

Stuck in Los Angeles, weaving my way between stubborn drivers and loud horns in bumper to bumper to traffic, time got the best of me. I sat at a standstill for hours, smiling about the frisky morning events, and thinking to myself, *'That was one for the books.'*

Begging to switch lanes, I met eyes with a few lookers. One in particular reminded me of Dean Kelte. Sexy, late thirties with sandy brown hair, driving a white Mercedes coup. He flashed his pearly whites and tilted his sunglasses, giving me the go ahead to get in front of him.

A chill traveled throughout me, remembering the first time I sat in the front seat of the professor's car. Late one night after a tutoring session, Professor Kelte gave his struggling students a ride to their dorms. When my classmate exited the car, I hopped in the front seat and lied about which Hall I lived in. "Where to?" He asked.

"How about your place? There's a lot more I need to learn," I said.

Kelte drove us back to his place faster than he drove to drop us off. I purposefully rose my plaid skirt to the top of my thighs, and placed his free hand on my leg. I didn't have to tell him what to do after I initiated. He pulled in the driveway of his rented house, "Please tell me this is real and you're not going to get me fired," he said.

I took his hand and placed it inside my bra. My nipples greeted him with a sharp tip. "I've seen the way you look at me in class. If you don't want this, take me home."

The look in his eyes screamed he wanted it. He wanted me. "I thought I would only have you in my dreams," he said.

"And how do you have me in these dreams of yours?" I unbuttoned my blouse.

"You said you have a lot to learn. Give me permission and I'll show you."

"I consent."

A horn blew on the 10, and my shoulders shook chills down through my hands. "Whew." I sighed. Thinking about my experiences with Dean Dick Me Down nearly made me miss the exit.

I swerved onto the ramp and safely arrived at my door. A few packages sat on the steps, next to a white petal that had fallen from the bouquet delivered to the house earlier. I inhaled its lingering lemon scent and my womanhood trembled. My mind revisited the way Rich tended to my petal hours ago, triggering me to dial his number and sort out this dilemma.

CHAPTER 8

Cause & Effect

R ich arrived at the back door dressed liked the average beach resident. Crisp white shirt, beige dockers, and overpriced brown leather flip flops. He greeted me with an elongated, tender kiss, then removed his shoes and tracked minimal sand from between his toes on the hardwood. He grabbed me from behind and kissed my neck. "I thought about you all day," he said.

I placed my hand on top of his, clutching my abdomen. "I can tell," I said, feeling him sprout between my cheeks.

"How was your day? You took forever to call to say you loved the flowers."

"Sorry about that. I went into the city and experienced L.A. traffic. It took me forever to make it back."

"I was hoping to hear from you sooner. I had plans to take you out to a romantic dinner in the city tonight. Are you free tomorrow?" Rich pecked a line of kisses from my neck to the edge of my shoulder.

"I am, but there's something you should know before you make plans."

The kisses stopped short of traveling down my arms. He

frowned and stepped back, then reached for both of my hands. "Your tone says something's up. What is it?"

I concealed my lips, then let go of his hands. "Your son saw us this morning."

"Impossible. He didn't get home until mid-morning. I wouldn't have put you on display if he were home."

"We were so engrossed in the moment we didn't hear him come in. He saw us. He came by here and told me to stop seeing you." I sighed.

Rich scoffed.

"There's more," I said. "You should know your son has an issue with me because I confessed I was into you, and things got slightly heated between us the night we went out."

"Are you trying to tell me you fucked my son and then me?"

"No. But I'm curious to know how you'd feel if I had." I stood to the side on one leg and placed my hand on my hip.

Rich looked befuddled. He took his time to calculate a response, puckering his lips and wrinkling his forehead. "Well?" I asked.

"Well I'm glad you didn't, so I don't have to think about it anymore."

"You okay—With me—Or?"

"I am." He grinned. "I mean we're just having fun, right?"

"Right. I leave in a few weeks and we fucked once, so we can kill this serious vibe going on in here. I apologize if my telling you any of this killed the momentum from when you arrived. If you'd like we can order in, or we can chill tonight. It's totally up to you."

"I get the feeling I need to take care of the situation back at my house. How about I call you tomorrow and take it from there?"

"Sounds good."

Rich showed himself the door and never called the next

day. Or the day after. The romantic dinner in the city never happened, and the only time I saw him was during my erotic dreams. I yearned for him sometimes during the day, but mainly at night when his shadow trailed me from the corners of every room. His presence was so strong I could still feel him thrusting and touching me from nearly a week after our early morning rendezvous. And when I'd wake, four syllables always came to mind. *Fucking Derrick.*

Mom called to check on me. Like normal, I sent her call to voicemail. When I played it, she said the same thing as always. "I sensed something was wrong." Mom and her senses. I've never been able to escape those maternal itches of hers, or her fiending to live vicariously through me and get *all* in my business. Then she dropped a gem. "Also, one of your professors from school called and asked for you to contact him. Something about your math portfolio. His name was Kels, or Ken, or something along those lines. Oh well. Call me."

A mild, wicked laugh escaped my lips while listening to my mother's message. *Dean Kelte was looking for me.* Sinfully I grinned and exhaled to catch my breath. If I knew any better, he was already close by, and I wondered how long it would be before he tracked me down and showed up at my doorstep. Tick tock.

CHAPTER 9

Yellow

After a week of not hearing from Rich, I stopped counting the days, and used my free time to hang the paintings and accents on the freshly painted bare walls. To avoid an awkward encounter with either of The Donovans, I skipped going down to the beach and relaxed on the balcony. As the chills hit me night after night, I had an epiphany to add an outdoor firepit.

A new set of contractors arrived to the house, fulfilling my request within four days. I sat outside enjoying the cool breeze, next to a warm fire with a glass of wine for days after it was installed. The space was tranquil, providing a place to think and plan to grow my business. Also, the place where I met Chase, the Inspection Specialist.

Chase was direct in his approach. He came and verified all of the building codes were met on the firepit, tested its safety, and approved its installation. He signed the documentation required for the city records, then passed his clipboard over to me. "Miss, if you'll have a look at this," he said. I reached for the papers and his fingers lingered with mine. He smiled and said, "Keep it as the first love letter of many more to come."

I blushed from his subtlety and sweetness. "I'm flattered. I truly am. But I don't want to ruin a good guy like yourself for someone who deserves you. I'm fresh on the rebound. Actually, I'm not even sure what I have going is over. You don't deserve to be involved in my mess," I said.

"You're right. But if you change your mind or just want to go out for a drink and talk about whatever it is you have going on, give me a call."

I took his card and studied the topaz color of his face, struggling to pinpoint his origin. He was beautiful, and kind. Not a part of my plan, but impressive. Appearing in my dream without a summons. Adding to the ménage I envisioned of me on my hands and knees with Dean Kelte ramming me from behind and Rich fucking my face. Chase entered the special dream knowing where he was needed. Below me with one nipple in his mouth, one hand on the other, and one finger on my clit.

The next morning, I woke with drenched sheets and an insurgence for the touch of a man. It'd been two weeks since I was embraced and caressed, and Chase's offer came calling soon after loneliness cradled me one cold night by the fire.

He arrived with takeout and a listening ear. A true gentleman he was. Completely opposite of what I was used to. A contrast to my deep desires.

As the fire crackled and the breeze from the ocean swirled around us on the balcony, I captured Chase smiling down at me. My wool wrap kept me comfy on the cushioned daybed as he sat opposite me. Heeding every word that spilled from my mouth. "You care to go for a walk out there?"

"Not tonight," I said. "It was kind of you to come over and keep me company. Suddenly I'm embarrassed about my champagne problems. I must sound shallow."

"You sound no different from my sisters," he said. "I'll tell you what I tell them. Don't lump us all in the same pile."

"I'll try and remember that." I giggled. "Shall we do this another time?"

"I hope so."

As Chase was on his way out, he stepped outside the door and took my hand. "Whoever the guy is—he's a fool not to be here right now. I hope I get to see you again before you leave town. Maybe even give you a reason to stay. You have a good night."

He kissed me on the cheek and I held in my chuckle. While he was being noble, I was imagining having my way with him to satisfy the lustful pleasures that weren't being met. I closed the door and leaned against it, guilty I fed him a falsehood of who I truly was. Far from the good girl he thought he saw in me. Definitely not the wholesome woman he needed or was looking for.

I returned to the balcony to clean up and turn off the pit. A yellow rose on a long stem fell next to my feet. Then another. And another. I peeped over the balcony where Rich stood holding a bag in one hand, and the remaining batch of roses in the other. His eyebrows raised and I scoffed before disappearing from his view to go back inside. Another rose fell behind me near the pit. I threw it back over the balcony, went into the house, and turned off the light.

While removing my makeup, I heard Rich knocking on the back door. I smiled at myself in the mirror, laughing inside as I left him out there in the cold. When he stopped, my face grimaced in the mirror and I stood there in a daze, confused of what I wanted.

My thoughts finally cleared and I changed into my gown, noticing how it resembled the dress Rich bought me. I slipped out of it, and jumped at the sound of the bell ringing at the front door. The hair on my neck raised as I stood half naked in my bedroom contemplating what to do. Then a chill froze my nipples, and the pulse between my thighs grew unbearable to ignore. I slipped down the stairs and looked through the window. *Of course, it's him.*

CHAPTER 10

The Unsaid

There he stood mysterious in the dark, but his puppy eyes gleamed from the surrounding lights, bouncing off the glass of the hanging pot of plants above the porch bench. I opened the door in my panties. He smiled and hurried inside looking over his shoulder and pushing me out of the door's view. The door shut and his gaze aroused me, staring at me like a statue in an art class. The bag and bouquet fell to the floor and he leapt towards me, grabbed my face and intensely gazed into my eyes.

The house was so still, I could hear his heart pounding as we challenged each other not to blink for nearly a full minute. I caved first. Then his lips met mine with a delicate, wet kiss.

I welcomed the rush of his caress, brushing my hands against his shoulders. Rich passionately tasted my skin. My chin. My neck. My breasts. I moaned at the technique of his hands applying pressure in the right places—Lessening on gentler zones, then tightening where my body called to be gripped.

Quickly he turned me around. My face pressed against

the wall accepting every lick he delivered down my back, to in between the slot of my cheeks where he paused. He moved the thin fabric of my thong to the side, and tucked his tongue inside my dark tunnel. I whined and wriggled, then gasped aloud as he continued traveling to my southern hemisphere, holding me open as my back arched to allow him access to taste me.

His foreplay was swift. Rich penetrated my orifice and fucked me like a soldier arriving home after a year-long tour. I wailed while smiling at my punishment. No longer craving his touch, but wanting it to never end instead.

He grunted after each stroke inside my pussy. The sound of his sighs made me wetter. And when I came from the urgency of his lashing, the head of his penis jerked and expanded inside me. His deep grunts elevated to tenor with shrieks of a soprano, while the tight grasp he held around the back of my neck held me in place for the taking. And I took, and took until he stroked his relief inside my walls.

With one hand he held me up against the wall from the middle of my back. I heard the rustle of his pants rise and zipper connect. Briefly the presence of his hand disappeared and I attempted to turn to face him. He pressed me back against the wall as I heard the bag crackle then fall to the floor again. A click sounded behind my ear, followed by the warm clatter of beads roving up my back then around my neck.

Rich placed his hand under my hair and shifted my tresses aside, then fastened the latch of a necklace with one pearl centered on a gold string. He turned me around and ran his hands along the line of where the pearl rested, then kissed me goodbye.

I watched him walk up the street towards his house with his hands in his pocket from the window of the foyer, fondling the jewel between my fingers. Not one word was spoken, but a lot was said in those quick five minutes of midnight delight.

I picked up the bouquet and placed them inside an empty vase stashed above the refrigerator. In the middle of the greenery, a clip held the card.

A woman like you deserves a full strand,
but until then, accept this single pearl.
I will add more in the years to come.

P.S. I think of the first pearl necklace
I gave you every night.
~Rich

I returned upstairs and slipped in the nighty I abandoned, and slept with my hands between my legs, rubbing the pearl until I fell asleep. In the morning I crossed off the days remaining until my uncle returned on the calendar in the pantry.

A few final tasks remained before the upgrade was completed, and with time winding down, I was forced to act on finalizing decisions for the dining room. A quick one-hour drive to Santa Barbara fixed my quandary, with upscale shoppes I wish I'd visited before dealing with the hassle of online deliveries.

The coastline was beautiful. Overflowing views of a rocky, blue ocean, palm tree filled towns, artsy cafes, and dining villas with the Santa Ynez Mountains as the backdrop. I felt myself becoming attached to the region, dreading the end of a ritzy life I pretended was mine. But as I returned with a car load of finds, food, and trinkets to unpack, a visitor awaited and I was reminded of where I came from, and could possibly return.

"I was wondering when you would show up."

CHAPTER 11

The Professor

Tall and broad shouldered with a five o'clock shadow stood Dean Kelte. His white polo shirt and fitted blue jeans did him justice. He always looked cute outside of his sweater vests, blazers, and slacks, but in street clothing he was a babe.

I was sure he knew this, hence showing up in casual gear. "You've been quite the busy girl," he said. One thing I learned from him was when to speak, and when to let others talk themselves in a hole. "I counted three guys I believe. Or is my competition steeper?" Kelte's lips curled at me while removing his sunglasses.

"What are you doing here Kel?"

"I haven't heard from you since graduation. Wondered how you were getting along, being that you were still looking for work when you left."

"And now that you've found me, are you still wondering how I'm getting along?" I narrowed my eyes at him.

"Oh no. I can see everything is coming along for you quite nicely."

Kelte placed the stem of his glasses in his mouth and

swept over me with his eyes head to toe. I shook my head and scoffed, "You want to be invited inside I presume?"

"Thought you'd never ask." He squeezed my ass.

I dropped my head, expecting nothing less from him, and pointed to the back seat. He took a few trips back and forth, fully unloading the car, then toured the house while I organized my latest finds in the proper rooms. A text from Chase chimed on my phone.

I'd love to see you. Will you join me for dinner tonight? It's Chase by the way.

I answered, "Yes," after I messaged Rich a "*Thank You*" text that went unanswered.

After Kelte examined the house, he joined me in the kitchen. "Aren't you going to offer me a drink?" His voice lingered.

"Would you like your usual?" I made eyes at him.

"If you'll join me."

I poured us a tinge of scotch in the new glasses I purchased for my uncle's lounge table in the den. Kelte sipped slowly, assaying my growth since we last saw each other. He was stalling to reveal why he was really visiting me. "Why haven't I heard from you? My number is still the same."

"I told you—You would hear from me if or when necessary." I sassed him.

"Humph. It would appear I've been replaced. Who are your new gentleman friends?" He ogled me until I replied.

"Jealous?" I pressed my top teeth into my bottom lip.

"Should I be?" His brows raised.

"Perhaps?" I shrugged. "Now why are you here?"

Kelte stalled with another sip, widening his mouth and clearing his throat from the strength of the scotch. I tapped my feet with my arms folded, hurrying him to answer me. "I was offered a position at UCLA. I called to invite you out here with me, but someone changed their number." He eased his way from around the counter over to me. "I've missed looking into those brown eyes." He deflected.

"How did you get my mother to tell you where I am?"

"Your mom loves flattery. She was also eager to hear I landed you a position alongside me at the university."

"Let me guess. Your Teacher's Assistant."

He moistened his thin lips and smiled. "I've accepted the job. Now say you'll work under—I mean with me." A devilish chuckle escaped his throat. *He meant under.*

"Professor, I've graduated. From school and you."

"You mean the banker? Or the contractor?"

My eyes enlarged. "How do you know their professions?"

He pursed his lips and placed his arms around me. "You're so cute when you pretend you don't like my meddling. You know you missed me. Now tell me, which one is your favorite?" He traced my lips with his finger. "Do either of them fuck you like I do? And remember. I've been watching."

"Yes." My voice softened.

"Which one?"

"I don't owe you any answers."

I stared into his devilishly defiant eyes and escaped his embrace. He drew me in closer and secured me with a bear hug. I gasped at the sudden tug and he kissed my parted lips, squeezing me so tight I grew limp.

The taste of his tongue was still the same. Fresh and minty. The seductiveness of his presence elevated. The desire I had for him. Still existent. "Tell me what you want?" Kelte lowered his hands to my ass and pressed his print firm against my womanhood. "You want me to make you pearl? Don't you? Say it." He demanded.

"Where are you staying?" I asked.

He forced his bulge deeper, hunching me into the fridge. My pussy vibrated and my back shivered. Kelte smirked looking down at me. He eased his hand inside my leggings and slid his finger on top of my clitoris, then held it there until I sighed. "At a house on campus. But I thought I could stay here tonight," he said.

"Professor Kelte, you can't stay here." I moaned, falling into his trap.

"You can do better than that Miss Edmonds. I want you to come like you did last night. But harder."

I wanted to so bad. The professor knew when, where, and how to get me off with the flick of a finger. "God, I want to," I panted. "But stop. I have a date I need to get ready for." I twisted my way out of his control, and removed his hand.

"With which one?" His mouth pursed as if my plans were of no importance.

"Again. My business." I led him towards the door.

"C'mon. Cancel your plans. I'll cook us breakfast. We both know you'll be too weak to do it." He smiled, stroking my cheek.

"It was nice seeing you Kel. I'll call you."

Kelte palmed my pussy with one hand, and pinched my nipple through my t-shirt. "I know you will." My tunnel muscles contracted, kegeling by his grip.

"Professor that's enough," I whispered.

He shied away at my command. It was good to see he still followed the rules. "There's a faculty function at The Ritz in Marina del Rey this weekend. Be my date. I'll get us a room and we can pick up where we left off." He kissed the back of my hand.

"Send me the details. I'll think about it," I said.

CHAPTER 12

The Date

Chase proved to be a huge surprise and breath of fresh air. He went from the stained shirt, tool belt wearing stranger, to the sweatshirt listening friend on the balcony, to a sexy sweater wearing piece of eye candy.

The brandy colored V-neck pullover blended beautifully with his complexion, but also teased his sculpted chest and iron pumped biceps. A sight to devour in the dimly lit booth of the restaurant he chose for our date. "This place has the best food. Order whatever you want. I promise you'll love it," he said.

He was beyond enthusiastic about this place. I couldn't help but smile at the excitement in his eyes when he ordered barbecue shrimp for the table, a filet mignon medium rare, mashed potatoes, and apple crumble for dessert. He caught my gaze. "What?" He parted his full lips and smiled.

"Nothing," I replied, blushing from my stares. "I'll have the same except with sweet potatoes."

"Excellent choice," said the waitress.

He reached over the table. "May I," he asked, taking my menu to hand to the waitress, gawking at him like she was in love. I didn't blame her. He was enchanting me as well with his kindness and manners—his consideration, and how fucking gorgeous his skin looked in the ochre lighting.

"Seems I have some competition." I teased.

He blushed. "Not at all. My sights are on you and you only."

"So, you're completely unattached? No ex-girlfriends looming around?"

"I have past relationships, but none looming around as you put it." He adjusted himself in his seat.

"May I ask you a hypothetical question?" My eyes lowered.

"Shoot." He lifted the glass of water in front of him to his mouth.

"Have you or would you share a woman?"

Chase choked and wrinkled his forehead. After clearing his passage, he leaned in towards me and whispered, "Do I seem like that kind of guy?"

"Far from it. Which makes me wonder."

"May I ask, where did *that* question come from?" He patted his chest.

"I had a dream about you the other night—after you left. I've never participated in a threesome before, but in this dream, I was the center of attention in a foursome, and you were there. Holding me and asking if I was alright throughout the ordeal. Almost like protecting me during this naughty affair, but enjoying the show of me being pleasured."

He sat back and glanced at my hardened nipples then sighed. His eyes shifted from my breasts and searched around the room. A moment of silence crossed us as the waitress returned to fill his glass. After she scurried off he stammered, "Is that something you want to experience in real time?"

"I'm curious yes. But..."

"But what?"

"Not if it would cause me to lose out on love." I stared into his eyes. "I'm only bringing it up because you were in the dream. So, would you...if I were to ask?"

Chase took another sip from the glass. He released an "Ahh,"as if he had been drinking a soda. "I'm selfish Amber. What's mine is mine. But—if the situation were to arise, and you were up front about it like you are now—I could be interested."

"I'm not convinced." I giggled.

"Because I hope I don't have to share you."

He wiped the uncomfortable smile from his face and stared at me intensely. "The day we met, you said I shouldn't get involved in your crazy life. Is this what you were talking about?"

"Kind of."

"You know when I asked you here tonight, I was hoping you had all of that sorted out." He placed his hand on top of mine.

"I'm this close," I gestured with my thumb and index finger. "Why? Is there a reason I need to resolve my issues under a time table?"

"I thought we hit it off the other night. I was hoping you could leave your drama behind, and give us a shot."

"My living situation is temporary here. You know this. I'd have to find a place of my own, land more clients. I'm still building my brand."

"If you choose to stay, I have all that worked out. There's something I want to show you after dinner." His eyes sparkled.

"And here I was thinking my dream would have scared you off, and you'd be calling for the check by now." I scoffed.

"Your dream could be your subconscious telling you I do want to hold you. And protect you. But also make sure you're good in my hands."

I wiggled in my seat. Moisture saturated my panties from his nonsexual word play. If I had been paying for our meal, I would have hailed for the check right then.

My suggestive topic didn't ruin our date. I complimented him on the excellent restaurant choice. "This is the best meal I've had since arriving out west," I said.

"Stick with me. You'll have the best of everything life has to offer." He winked. "How was your trip today?"

An image of Kelte grinding up against me popped into my head. I shook it off and answered, "I fell in love. I would love to live in Santa Barbara one day. Malibu is gorgeous, don't get me wrong, but there was something breathtaking about Barbs. The views during my drive were spectacular. I hate I didn't get to take pictures. I definitely want to spend more than a few hours there next time."

"How about I take you?" He offered.

"I think I'd like that."

After dinner, Chase drove me to the mystery place he mentioned. He guided the steering wheel with the palm of his hand into a parking space in front of a beige colored apartment building. "Where are we?" I asked.

"This is Cornell," he said. "This is what I wanted to show you."

He hopped out of the car and took me by the hand. As he pulled out a set of keys and opened the door to a dark, stuffy apartment, my voice cracked. "Is this your place?"

"Ugh. Something like that," he stammered. "I inherited the building actually. If you choose to stay, the place is yours."

I looked at him confused. "Chase, honestly you don't have to do this."

"I want to."

"I'd be foolish to lock myself into a leasing agreement right now."

"It's my place. Why would I charge you rent?"

My face turned flush pink and blank. I observed the apartment with ideas popping up of how I could spruce it up. A chair here, a painting there. "I didn't bring you here to freak you out. I just wanted you to see it before you decide to leave Cali." Chase explained holding up his hands.

"Thank you. It's a lovely place. I could bring it to life. Can I think on it?"

"Of course." His voice dragged.

"So, where do you live?"

"A few miles from here. C'mon. I'll show you my place."

He took me by the hand and escorted me back to the car. We drove a few blocks in silence. Sporadically he peeked at me during red lights, and when I sang random parts to the song on the radio. A few minutes later we arrived in a regal neighborhood, different from most of what I had seen on the coast.

In most areas, houses were stacked on top of each other with little room to breathe, or a private yard. This neighborhood had space between the homes, pools in the backyard, and privacy between them. *'Business must be good,'* I thought.

The garage lifted on a two-story ranch style home. "This is me," he said. "It's not the beach, but it's home."

He gave me the tour of *his* place. I followed him around searching for photographs of a family, or proof of any kind he was possibly house sitting for someone. *A common scheme in Lala Land.* But there it was. Pictures of him on the mantle above the fireplace. "This has to be your father," I said.

"Yeah, that's my Papi. Descansa en paz." Chase kissed two fingers and raised them to the sky.

"Papi, huh." I poked out my lips. "Are you ever going to tell me your nationality?"

"I'm Cuban."

"Ha! Finally, I can stop guessing."

He shook his head grinning at me from the entrance of the hallway. "C'mon. See the rest of the place." He nodded his head.

"I have a lot of questions, but I don't want to put my foot in my mouth."

"Go ahead. Ask me whatever." He swung my hand back and forth, then stopped outside of his bedroom.

"How?" I held up my hands.

"First hard work. Second, my dad saw to it I was comfortable if anything ever happened to him. I took over his business and here I am."

"Impressive." My brows raised.

"Any more questions?" He faced me and linked his fingers with mine.

"Did you bring me here because of my revelation at dinner?"

Chase pulled me in close and we kissed. "What happens if I say yes?" He stole my lips once more, then lured my tongue into his mouth. It was just as enticing as I'd imagined. Heat ran through my body as he took me in his arms and pressed my ass into his cock. It throbbed and so did I. Sighing for it to be inside of me.

He carried me into his bedroom and laid me on his bed. A different demeanor overwhelmed him. His face transformed from the kind person I had spent the past couple of hours with, to the sexy beast who infiltrated my dream. "I want to warn you. What I'm about to do to you—is fuck up your life. In a good way. Think you can manage?"

I nodded, but was thinking, *'The fuck?'* as he undressed completely and stood before me pulling on his glorious, tanned, downward curved nature. *'Oh boy,'* I thought.

Hovering over me, the look in his eyes made me wet. My

lips parted and he kissed them delicately, then stood holding his weapon at the base. "Do you suck Amber?" My reply was a simple grin. "I want you to suck me when I tell you too. Alright?"

"Okay." I answered while thinking, '*Who is this motherfucker?*'

CHAPTER 13

Chase

My nipples turned hard as ice and pebbled in his mouth. My pussy ached of curiosity and thrusted upwards towards his raging, rigid cock. My blouse hugged my waist until he pulled it past my thighs simultaneously with my jeans and bikini.

He stood and placed my panties to his nose. "These are mine now."

One by one he removed my pumps and held my legs in the air, squeezing my calves, and kissing my feet. I squealed from the first lick to my instep, then shrieked as he rolled his tongue across my toes, gently sucking each one as he stared into my eyes. Again, I asked myself. '*Who is he and where did this side to him hide in the daytime?*'

His tongue glided up my leg and stopped short at my peak. He straightened his back with his dick in my face upright and long. "Spread those legs wider so I can feel that pussy."

I opened myself for him and leaned my head back from the circular rub of his fingers.

"How long have you been wet for me baby?"

"All night." I sighed with my eyes closed.

"Open those pretty eyes for me."

I shifted my head forward and followed his command.

"Open your mouth." His voice shook my soul.

I parted my lips and welcomed his cock on my tongue. Slowly, he rocked his hips forward then rolled them, brushing his head at the roof of my mouth. I traced it and squeezed it with my jaws.

He moaned. "Yes. That's it. Just like that," rolling it around the entrance of my throat. He pulled it out, and slipped a swift kiss to my lips. "You like that?"

"Yeah." I giggled. "Did you?"

"Oh, I love it baby. Trust me, we're far from done." He dropped to his knees and spanked my slit. "Let's see if it's as sweet as I think it is."

My southern lips pulsed for his to taste them. He obliged softly at first, swirling his tongue around my orifice like it was ice cream, pausing in between kisses and sucked on my clit.

The sound of slurps, the excitement of finger taps, and the urgency of where his mouth was going to explore next made me shout, "Please don't stop!" He hummed as he continued withdrawing from my fountain. The soft slow sensual lick fest turned into a tongue lashing. Chase stuck his long tongue inside my cave and rolled it in waves against the top of my nook. I clung to the sheets, screaming his name, then he stopped.

I looked up as my body flipped, hanging half off of the bed.

"On your knees," he said.

I crawled on my hands while he assisted in helping me assume the desired position by lifting my ass until my knees were close to the edge. A long, hard lick traveled from my clit. My body tensed and I dropped my head between my hands on the bed, while his tongue waved again, this time against my folds.

I rained in his mouth, struggling to hold my position as my legs shivered. His tongue then reinserted inside my pussy and waved again. This time on the bottom of my tunnel. My moans muffled against the bedding.

"You want me to stop?" he teased.

"Please don't. I beg you."

A wicked gurgle vibrated against my folds before he tongue-fucked me with sturdy strides.

He came up for air. "You know you're mine now, right?"

I could see in his eyes it annoyed him that I didn't answer. He dove and licked my *Silk Road*, circling my button with his tongue. My ass bounced in his hands holding it steady. His fingers gripped my cheeks and suddenly I shuddered from the shock of his wet tongue circling my asshole.

I cried out, "Chase."

He showed me mercy, sliding it inside of my dark tunnel, waving it like the red flag I knew he was.

My pussy throbbed and contracted as I begged him, "Please Chase! Fuck me now! Please!" His curved penis slid inside my walls. I squeezed them and held him tight, then loosened my muscle, sighing from the pleasure.

As he felt my flesh retracting, he fucked me hard, fast, and deep. My fist pounded against the bed. My mouth opened from his delightful, surprising fuckery.

"You love this dick babe?" He rolled his hips and smacked my ass.

"I do." I whined.

"You got some good pussy baby. I knew you had a diamond mine." He breathed out, then smacked my ass again. "Spit those diamonds for me," he shouted, long dicking me from behind.

I buried my face into the sheets I uncovered from clawing

away on the bed. Hollering. Smiling. Cock-eyed. The hook from the tip of his dick thrusted against a zone never explored. I assumed it was the love zone because I held my tongue from shouting 'I love you!' as he plowed me like an oil rig. Instead I moaned his name. "Chase!"

"You're taking this dick real good baby. I'm proud of you." He sighed as he grunted.

He placed his feet next to mine on the bed, held me by my waist, and hunched over me, digging further into the top of my passage. The heavens heard me call from the muffles I screamed into the mattress.

"You're a soldier," he tittered, tracing my asshole with his thumb while grinding my pussy with his balls rubbing on my clit.

I creamed on his dick.

"That's it babe. Cream-pie my dick." He *grinded* until my convulsions ceased.

Briefly, he allowed me to enjoy my climax, tracing my back with his tongue until he reached my neck. Standing over me on the bed, he placed his forearm below my stomach and turned me over. I lied on my back and stared at him in amazement. He grinned then backed away from the bed, sliding me to the edge closer to him. "My Papi," I sighed, as my wild lover pulled me up by my hands, then placed one of his fingers in my mouth.

"Your turn," he said, stroking his shotgun ready to shoot.

His fingers left my mouth and grabbed my hair into a ponytail. He fed his tip to my lips and I gripped his head with the front of my mouth. Sliding my lips back and forth on the neck of his head.

He groaned, easing his cock in small strokes on my tongue. "Open up," he ordered.

I obeyed and opened my mouth wide, and stuck my tongue down past my bottom lip. Chase's other hand cupped my throat and face fucked me hardcore, ringing the bell on my tonsils until I gagged.

He pulled out and mouthed. "You alright?"

I nodded.

"One more time darling." His finger brushed the side of my lip before he returned his cock to my mouth. Fast pumps, in and out led him to whisper, "Good girl, Amber. Yes. Taste that sweet pussy of yours."

I spread my fingers wide on his thighs, taking the lashing until he tired out.

He pulled out and wiped the drippings from my chin. "You like that, did you?"

I looked up at him and smiled.

He grinned. "Fuck them other clowns. You're mine. You hear me."

I snickered and lied on my back.

Chase tasted my pearling tongue with his once more, then stuck his cock back in my pussy. He lifted my legs and scraped my flesh into submission with that curve of his. I held him at bay by his shoulders, but he was too strong and overpowered my hold.

He leaned forward and kissed me, moaning how good I felt beneath him. "You good?"

"Mmm hmm." I pined.

"You know you're mine, right?"

"Yes." I played along.

He pulled out and lifted me, then rubbed his tip across my lips. "I dreamed of you sucking me off, but you feel too good. I have to go back in."

My legs swung over his head. He lunged back inside and stood up in my pussy, tightly scraping inside as he massaged my ass cheeks. The tight friction rendered howls until he boisterously came and spat his warm seeds on my ass.

His legs locked and he jolted until he was empty, then he

spread my ass open and softly kissed my pussy in counts of three until I finished trembling.

"Mmm." He moaned and hummed, licking me clean as I lost motion in my legs.

Out of breath he fell beside me and pulled me in close, breathing heavily in my ear. Once he collected himself he said, "If a man had to choose his death, I would definitely choose to die fucking you Amber Edmonds."

CHAPTER 14

Two Glasses & A Bottle of Bourbon

I was fucked. Figuratively and literally. I've shared some wild nights with the professor, but my first night with Chase cast some sort of magic erasure spell. Well, at least while I was lying next to him. How I was able to sleep peacefully and sound in a strange house threw me for a loop. But then again, he did ride me into temporary paralysis.

I woke up to Chase's face between my legs, tending to my garden for breakfast with a slow, romantic, sensual tonguing. He climbed on top of me and made love to my breast with his mouth, then wiggled himself inside my passion pit. Easy this time.

Staring into my eyes, he stroked a deep mid-tempo rhythm. His lips nibbled my neck while my hands pressed into the back of his shoulders. I held my breath every time I inhaled, waiting for the beast from the night before to unleash upon me. But he never showed. He tenderly caressed my bum with each hand, lifting my pussy upward and side to side, digging into my corners.

The soreness welcomed the pain of his penis, morphing into a pleasurable remedy as he painted my wet canvas with his paintbrush. And when he came, his orgasm mimicked that of a quiet cry. He pressed his cock to the back of my canal and stayed there until my cup *runneth* over.

"Good morning," he said.

"Good morning," I whispered.

"Spend the day with me. We can do whatever you want. Take that trip to Santa Barbara, or do this." He growled, rubbing the side of my waist and nipping my lobe.

"There is no way you still have another one in the chamber." My brows raised.

"You're funny." Chase laughed. "But sweetheart, I could make love to you all day and all night."

Judging from the sexy, serious gaze on his face, I believed him. I placed the covers over my head and we wrestled beneath the sheets. "I'd love a shower. Some food. And rest. But I have to be home this evening." I softly said stroking his chest.

"Well until then, you're mine."

He fed me. And bathed me. And clothed me with one of his t-shirts while I lounged around his house. My head rested in his lap on the couch as we napped until it was time for him to drive me home.

When we arrived back in Malibu, he walked me to the door, and kissed me passionately for the entire neighborhood to see.

"I'll give you a few days to iron out your wrinkles. But please call me if you need me." He kissed the back of my hand.

"I can take care of myself. Don't worry." I pinched his cheeks.

"My bed is going to miss you in it. I might have to come scoop you up later on tonight. And I won't take no for an answer." He squeezed my ass and tickled my neck until I squealed.

Laughter from within the house caused me to jump while I was in Chase's arms. "Wait here," he said. "I'll go check it out."

"No need. It sounds like my uncle." I pulled on his arm.

"I'll come with you to make sure."

Pacing a few steps in front of me, Chase followed the voices into the den. Two glasses and a bottle of bourbon rested on the coffee table, and a streaming of the Nasdaq report played in the background. "Amber! My love! Where have you been all night?" Uncle Jeff hopped up from the leather lounge chair. "You remember my golf buddy Rich. I called him over to see what you've done with the place."

"Uncle Jeff. You're back early." I gave him a hug and eyed Rich over his shoulder. Rich acknowledged me with a nod and gave Chase a once over.

"Yeah. A storm hit the resort in Bangkok my travel agent reserved, so I had two choices. Take my chances in places I hadn't researched, or come home early and spend the last days of my vacation in my new place. I'd say I chose wisely."

"Bummer about the storm." I said through my teeth. "But it's good you're back!" My voice livened.

"I tried calling you last night when I got in, but kept getting your voicemail."

I squirmed as Uncle Jeff outed me for having my phone off during my rendezvous with Chase. "Really?" I furrowed my brows and tilted my head.

"I wanted to commend you on the amazing job you've done with the house. We're going to have to sit down and talk about finding you some investors to go into business. You're good at this. I'm so proud of you."

Second time I've heard that in a day.

Chase and I made eyes then grinned at each other. My uncle squeezed my shoulders and turned towards him. "Who's your friend?"

"Chase Alonso, meet my uncle, Jeff Edmonds. The reason I'm in California. Uncle Jeff, meet …"

Chase interrupted me and raised his hand, "It's nice to meet you sir."

"Likewise." Uncle Jeff leered at him slightly before shaking his hand. "Care to join us for a drink?"

"No sir. I'm driving and on my way to take care of some business. Maybe another time?" He smiled at me.

"Sure son."

"I'll check on you later." Chase squeezed my hand. "Again, it was nice meeting you sir."

I beamed from his attention and respect for my family. He kissed my cheek, then briefly stared into my eyes before excusing himself. I twisted side to side and pretended to listen to the reporter call out numbers in the background, but could see Rich glaring in my direction until Uncle Jeff turned towards him. "Rich here was telling me things didn't work out between you and his son. I guess it's nice you met someone out here to keep you company. He seems like a nice young man." Rich shuffled in his seat and cleared his throat.

"Very nice," I said.

"Just as you were walking in, I was telling Rich I'm going to throw a party on Saturday night to show off my new pad. Could be a great networking opportunity for you."

"This Saturday?" I frowned.

The Professor's event is Saturday.

"Don't worry. I'll hire someone to take care of the plans."

"I've got to head out Jeff, but I'm looking forward to it myself." Rich stood and finished off his glass. "I'll see you both on Saturday."

"I'll walk you out," said Uncle Jeff.

He led the way yammering about caterers and invitation lists. I followed the two of them out of the den. Rich paused his steps when my uncle turned the corner, did an about face and kissed me, then covered his actions. "Yeah." he said. "I'll find the name of that woman who does those parties for my ex-wife."

I smirked on the way up to my room, and turned on the shower until the steam fogged the mirror. I closed my eyes and pictured Rich and I on the rocks, Professor Kelte's hands down my pants in the kitchen, and Chase fucking me into delirium mentally and physically. I had the hots for all of them, but nothing tangible to show for it except a swollen papaya consistently throbbing for one of them to be inside of me.

A decision had to be made to secure my future financially. I opened my eyes and examined the woman looking back at me in the frosted mirror, questioning if the game I was playing was worth it. But more importantly, if the one I longed for the most, was *the one* for me.

CHAPTER 15

Après Moi

Chase kept his word and swung back by the house for a few kisses, and questioning if I had given more thought about the apartment. I avoided answering him successfully. I also avoided a midnight quickie thanks to Uncle Jeff joining us outside on the porch to cock block. *He knew what he was doing.*

Friday, the morning before the house party, I texted Professor Kelte.

I need to see you now.
Get a luxury room at The Waldorf.
Reply with the room number.

Once I received a response from Kelte, I texted Rich with instructions to meet me.

I sat at the bar and sipped on a few Peachy Mint Juleps until Rich texted he arrived. I paid my tab and took the elevator to Room 523. Kelte opened the door with his chest hairs sticking from his low buttoned shirt. "I've been waiting for this call." He sank his teeth into his bottom lip and pulled me inside.

I texted Rich, '523', and made myself comfortable near the bar. "I assume you can cover this on the bill," I said. And poured two glasses of scotch. I handed him a glass and raised the volume on the television, switching the channel from sports, to one of the music stations.

"Cheers." He raised his glass as Rich knocked on the door.

"This isn't for me," I said.

I opened the door and passed Rich the scotch. "Nice to see you," he said. I gestured for him to come inside. He kissed my cheek, "I didn't think I would ever get another moment alone with you." I cleared my throat and looked over at Kelte. Rich lowered the glass from his mouth. "What's going on here?" He gulped hard on his sip and stared in confusion.

"Gentlemen, have a seat."

They leered at each other before sitting in the chairs by the window. "Close those for me." I said pointing to the curtains. "I asked you two here today, to face my past and my present, in order to move on with my future. I have adoration for you both, but the fun we've shared can't last forever."

"I beg to differ," said Kelte.

"You would say that Kel, which is why after today I am letting you go for good. You've been a part of my life since college, and while it was fun..."

"It was fucking amazing," he said.

"Okay, it was amazing. But I have nothing to show for it. And you, Rich. I wanted to be with you since the moment we met, but things didn't pan out as I had hoped. And when they finally did—Well it put you in an awkward position. I'm sorry for that. But I wouldn't take a moment of it back."

"Neither would I," said Rich.

"And your communication sucks. I have no idea how you feel about me. But I do know the both of you have enjoyed my pussy for free, and that stops after today."

Kelte stared deep beyond my eyes then smiled. Rich scratched the hair near his temple, slow to catch on. "Does that mean you are finally going to???" Kelte lifted his brows and grinned.

I stood before them and slipped the straps of my dress down my shoulders, exposing my nude body. My nipples stood at attention and as my southern lips twitched. "Today is all about catering to me. Your assignment is to please. My assignment is to indulge and enjoy your efforts, and competitiveness to eroticize my body. Are we understood?"

"I've been fiending to taste you for months. I'll go first," said Kelte.

"No," said Rich. "After me."

Rich grabbed my face and tasted the peach and mint flavors of my beverage. "Mmm," he moaned, rolling the palm of his hands in a circular motion around my nipples. "You *wanna* know how I feel about you? You drive me crazy," he said, then placed his supple lips on my breast.

The pressure he placed in the small of my back made me hot for him. I lifted my head and closed my eyes, enjoying the personal detail he paid attention to my unyielding nipples. The feel of his tongue circling them, then clamping down, diving his teeth into them until my body rippled.

I opened my eyes and met Kelte's. He pulled his unbuttoned shirt over his head and dropped his pants, full and engorged like I remembered. We shared a wicked smile and he walked over to join us. Rich's hands slid down my sides and caressed my hips. Kelte stood behind me and ran his fingers through my hair, then swept my tresses from my shoulder, kissing my warm skin delicately across my back.

When he arrived to the other side I jolted as Rich's mouth sucked on my clit.

Kelte lifted my arms and wrapped his around me, tweaking my nipples. "Hold still for him love," he said. The feel of extra hands upon me felt better than I had imagined. I regretted I hadn't done it sooner.

As Rich lubed me, digging his claws into my cheeks, Kelte's dick pressed between them. I moaned of anticipation. His fingers traced my lips before he turned my head to face him. He gazed into my eyes then kissed me. Twice before closing them once we locked lips. I reached for his face and embraced the moment for a short while, then ordered him. "Follow his lead."

Kelte dropped to his knees. Both men held my body upright as their tongues bathed me in both orifices. I held myself, squeezing my nipples and running my fingers up and down my neck. Rich rose to his feet and asked, "Are you ready for me?"

I nodded and tapped Kelte on the shoulder. We moved to the bed and Rich lied on his back with his knees against the edge. "Come sit on this dick baby." I climbed on his pole and slid down his hard cock. Leaning forward face to face we kissed, while Kelte finished sucking my back door with the rhythm of Rich's upward thrusts.

After so many years of experience, Kelte knew when I came and stopped sucking. He placed his hands on my ass and bounced me up and down on Rich's dick so I would continue to be fucked during my climax.

"Take that beating," Kelte murmured.

"You sure you want to give up this cock?" Rich asked.

"Shut the fuck up—both of you." I ordered.

"Let me taste it." Rich nudged for me to turn around.

I rotated my position to ride Rich in reverse on the edge of the bed. Rich rubbed his fingers around my folds and placed them in his mouth. "Mmm." Rich moaned and smacked his lips.

Kelte dropped to his knees and guided my body down on Rich's cock. He moved me up and down, licking my clit as I rode like a cowgirl. I exhaled loudly, "That's it," said Rich, squeezing my bum. His hands trailed over to my button. He rubbed it soft and slow with his thumb. "We never got to explore there, love." I looked at him over my shoulder and smiled.

"Speak for yourself," said Kelte.

"Just keep that dick rock hard for me," I said.

Kelte stood tall. "I'm ready to tend to your need," he said. Rich selfishly fucked me harder while The Professor stood over me rubbing his cock up and down. Impatience forced him to take matters into his own hands. He pulled me from on top of Rich and ran his fingers through my hair, down my face, and over my breasts.

Standing in his arms, he finger-fucked me and licked my neck, pinching my nipples as my thighs ached for his pressure. "You didn't want me to stop this the other day. Did you?" He asked. I shook my head side to side and whined, staring at the erotic crazed eyes that woke the sexual being in me.

Once I covered his fingers with my slick, he lifted me on his pipe. Up and down he stroked my drenched pussy. I held onto his shoulders, gasping from his girth. Rich watched us from the bed, "Bring her to me," he said.

"Not yet." Kelte refused.

"Play nice boys."

Kelte grunted and sighed, "I missed this golden pussy."

"I'm missing it now." Rich added.

"I wouldn't dare stretch my Princess." Kelte enforced.

I was up to try it for a second, but thinking about the word stretched killed that curiosity. "Fuck me on the bed Professor," I said. He paused his beating and laid me on my back, continuing his pillage. I grabbed Rich's coated penis and rubbed him slow and steady while he randomly kissed my body where he desired. His mouth found one nipple and his hand the other, while the free hand traveled to my clit, and massaged it while my pussy was being hard fucked by The Professor. "Don't either of you stop doing what you're doing until I come!" I expelled.

The explosion I felt inside needed to be placed inside a bottle and sold. I lost the battle of being drowned out by the music in the background. I only hoped the hotel didn't rent the rooms next to us. Forcefully I shuddered beneath both men, doing what they were told. Catering to me.

As euphoria owned my body, I suddenly felt generous. I licked my lips at Rich. "Let me take care of you," I said.

"That's right Princess. Take care of him. I didn't teach you to be selfish," said The Professor.

"You *gonna* let me fuck that pretty mouth?" Rich asked. "Come here."

He hovered above me on his knees and gently ran his fingers in my hair. As he placed his cock in my mouth, I heard him belt an "Ooh," from the warmth of my tongue. Holding his pipe down at the base, he fed his tip to my lips, trembling whenever I lifted my head up for him to go deeper. He kept it sensual and slow, gasping for air.

When he pulled it completely out I asked, "You want me to finish you off?" He nodded and slid me to the edge so my head could hang off the bed. I ordered Kelte to suck and fuck me like he did in his classroom closet while the janitor cleaned. He obliged and rotated his licks and strokes every ten seconds. Pounds fucked my pussy for ten juts, followed with sloppy wet kisses on repeat while I sucked off Rich— deep in my throat and massaging his balls.

The rotation was short lived as all three of us were excited from the pleasure floating in the room. Rich bust in my mouth like a cannon. I tightened my jaws and he called out my name. "Amber! My God! Amber!"

"Show him what I taught you Princess," said Kelte.

Once Rich fully emptied his clip, he retreated and looked down at me. I fucked with his head, looked him in his eyes, and blew a bubble with his jizz.

His eyes grew wide. "I love you," he said wiping the side of my mouth.

"We both do," said Kelte, roaring on top of me, blasting across my chest.

Kelte rubbed his cock in his cream, spreading it between my breast and jerked out the last of his remains, then slid me to the middle of the bed. I relaxed with each one at my side. Rubbing me. Caressing me. Massaging me. "I'm going to miss you both," I said.

"I'm not letting you go," said Kelte.

"You have to."

"I'll give you whatever you want." Kelte added. "Even share you with this guy from time to time. If that's what you want."

"What do you want?" Rich asked.

"To never want for anything. To know I'm safe and loved so much, I'll never have to ask for money or affection. I want a house to call my own. Shelter is very important to me. And I want to know what's going on in my partners mind. I don't want to worry. About anything. And I want to know I'm good at all times. I want to be happy."

"I can give you all of that and more." Rich offered.

I turned towards Rich and saw the truth in his eyes. He did wish to offer me everything I wanted, but I knew the cost, and the strain of that cost would eventually come in between us.

The Professor placed his arm around my waist. Breathing against the back of my neck. I expected him to stay quiet. He and I both knew he could only offer me a mistress life filled with getaways and deviant sexual escapades. Nothing more.

"If this really is goodbye, please, one more round." Kelte begged, nibbling on my ear. "But this time you cater to us."

"That wasn't the assignment." Rich rolled me on top of him. "Get dressed. You're leaving with me."

CHAPTER 16

Green

"Get in," said Rich. His voice ricocheted deep authority. I hopped in his car and stared at the bubbling vein on the side of his neck. The engine revved when he cranked the car. "What the fuck was that in there?" I bit my nails and continued to study his angry side. "That's how you wanted to say goodbye? To me?" He hit his chest.

"If I had my way I'd be saying good morning to you. Running with you at 5 a.m. And saying good night in your bed. Unfortunately, I can't have my way, so I'm moving on with someone I can do those things with," I said.

"It is unfortunate," he took a deep breath and narrowed his eyes.

His demeanor appeared to be calmer than when he forced me out of the hotel. I glared at him until he blinked. "How do you feel about me Rich?"

"Is that what this is about? Three little words."

"They aren't so little."

He wiped his face with his hands then placed them on the steering wheel. "I helped you escape that brute in there. If I didn't care about you, I would have walked away. It took everything in me to watch another man defile you like that. But it was your request. Plus, you looked smoking hot taking charge like that."

"Did I?"

"You did. But I would not have watched another man put his cock in that pretty mouth."

I turned away and grinned. *He'd die if he saw my mouth earlier this week.*

A horn blew from the parking lane. "Are you leaving!" An angry motorist shouted. Rich waved for him to keep scouting and turned my face towards him.

"You were right in there. I am in a tight spot, but Derrick is turning 25 soon. I promised he could stay with me until then."

"And then what? You and me can finally be together? Ignore the dirty looks from the neighbors? Ruin your friendship with my uncle?"

"What if I ask him permission to date you? Man to man."

"No." I cut him off. "Then you'll have lost a son and a friend. Just let this be the end. Okay?"

"I can't."

"Why?"

"Because I...You know why." He held my hand.

"And this is why I'm with someone else." I slid my hand away.

"That chump at the house the other day?"

I nodded. "That chump has offered one of his homes so I can stay in Cali, and constantly professes how much he wants me to be his lady. I wish you felt that way about me. Nice knowing you Rich." I leaned over and kissed his cheek.

Preparing for the party served as my excuse to avoid seeing Chase. His response knocked me back a bit. "You'll make it up to me tomorrow night," he said. I was all for his manhandling in the sack, but began to wonder how many times was he going to tell me I was his—And boss me around. Honestly, reservations crossed my mind about living in a space he owned. Again ownership.

If I had my way, I would skip town for a few days and hide out in Santa Barbara. Pretend I lived there permanently in a big house away from the coast, in a safe, quiet community where the locals traded fresh food and supported each other's business endeavors, and overlook the fact that I didn't belong amongst them. And if they turned me away I'd just get even with them and fuck their husbands.

"Amber. Amber." Uncle Jeff called.

I jumped and gasped at the foot of the bed. "Huh?" I held my chest.

"I've been standing here awhile. You were miles away from here. Is everything okay?"

"Just daydreaming." I smiled.

"Well you look beautiful. Just like my baby sister when she was your age. The guests will be arriving shortly. I want to make sure they get to meet the person responsible for this upgrade. More clients, more *moolah. Cha Ching.*" He winked.

"I'll be right down."

Either Uncle Jeff invited the entire neighborhood, or word traveled fast about free food and alcohol. *'Apparently the upper class is just as raunchy as the lower class,'* I thought to myself, watching them shout across the room, and guzzle the free drinks. Some even arrived in beach attire. One woman desperately showed off her new body job in a see-through coverall. I couldn't be mad at her though. She looked phenomenal. A part of me wanted to go over to her and pick her brain. See if she fucked any of the men standing in the living room. One in particular, Rich, keeping his date for the evening company.

My glance over at Rich didn't go unnoticed. Derrick

weaseled his way over to me. "Sorry doll. My dad finally came to his senses and hooked up with someone more suitable," he said.

"Suitable," I scoffed. "That's a funny word. Is it suitable for you to be over here gloating about your father's love life Derrick? I thought we moved past this." I tugged on my necklace.

"C'mon. Admit it. I see the hurt in your eyes."

I pressed my lips together and stared at Rich. When his eyes met mine, I curved the side of my lip. "You know what Derrick. You're right. I am hurt. I was in love with your father, but he and I will never know what kind of grand life we could have had together, because he chose his son over love." I turned to see his reaction.

Derrick's face frowned and his forehead wrinkled, but a smirk crossed his lips. I wasn't sure if he cared he stood in the way of his father's happiness, or found my confession for loving him humorous. "But no need to worry about me Derrick. As you can see, every last man in this room has their eyes glued to my ass. I'll have no problem landing on my feet." I said as Chase walked in.

He brushed Derrick with his shoulder then kissed my cheek, "Hey baby. You look gorgeous as fuck. Green is definitely your color. Who's this?" He eyed Derrick from head to toe.

"This is Derrick. One of the first people my uncle introduced me to when I arrived to Malibu. Derrick, this is my date Chase." I placed my hand on his chest and leaned against his arm.

"We'll work on that date title later on tonight. If you know what I mean." He kissed my lips and grabbed my ass.

"My uncle's over there." I whispered and wiggled from his grip.

"Nice to meet you," Derrick reached for Chase's hand.

Chase nodded and raised his brows. "Yeah," he said.

I tapped his hand and he lifted it halfway to meet Derrick's palm as my uncle and a man from the party interrupted our conversation. "Amber. This party has turned into a celebratory night for you. Mr. Coppin here is interested in hearing your ideas for his home."

"Homes." Mr. Coppin corrected him. "I have a home down the stretch, but I also have properties in Miami. Let's set a meeting."

"I would love a meeting." My face beamed as I shook his hand.

"Give her my secretary's number Jeff." He placed his hand on my uncle's shoulder. "I hope to hear from you before I leave town."

He scurried off with his glass of champagne and Uncle Jeff in his ear. Chase clenched his jaw and stared at Derrick with steely eyes. "If you'll excuse me," Derrick said. Chase shook his head and stepped in front of me.

"How long do we need to stay here? I'm ready to get you home."

"Home?" I scowled.

"Yeah home. Your side of the bed feels like ice." He smiled. "I promise it'll be on fire tonight."

"What if I asked for the early morning treatment. You know. Slow. Attentive. Mind-bending." I bit my lip and gazed into his eyes.

"Ask and you shall receive. Let's go up to your room." He looked up at me kissing the back of my hands and swung them between us.

"We can't go up there with all these people in the house. My uncle thinks the world of me. I'd never disrespect him like that."

"Your uncle doesn't know you how I know you." He

chuckled and I released his hands. "I'm kidding. Lighten up. I miss you is all."

"Why don't you go outside and cool off. I could use a drink right now."

I strutted over to the bar with damn near all eyes upon me. "A Cabernet please." I said, leaning on the rounded wooden edge of the bar. The attendant nodded.

I breathed out and composed myself tapping on the wood. The essence of a familiar scent caused the hairs on my arm to stand. "I'd like a mimosa." Rich raised his finger to the bartender.

My fingers rolled around the pearl centered below my throat. His eyes stared straight ahead, but I felt like they were examining me. "Beautiful dress you're wearing. Looks as if it was made just for you."

"Thank you. It was a gift." I said, taking my glass from the bartender's hand. I sipped. "You look like a mimosa kind of man."

"It pairs well with a certain kind of cocktail." He laughed. "Also, with pearls."

"Enjoy your date. I mean your night." I said, running my fingers across the pearl, then joined my uncle waving at me from across the room.

Two more neighbors arranged appointments for an upgrade. The joy of a budding, prosperous career and opportunity to prove myself as a sustainable businesswoman could have filled the room. And I imagined it did. I looked around at all the happy faces laughing and dancing with champagne flutes and skewers in their hands, but no trace of Chase among them.

A drunken neighbor stole the party's attention. As the circle turned their heads to laugh at the spectacle of the beach crowd, I broke free and searched the house for Chase.

My assumption he'd be waiting for me upstairs in my

bedroom proved false. I searched the balcony were I first entertained him. Empty. I flounced downstairs to the den. Still no luck. I thought, '*Maybe he left.*' I sighed, and footed up the hallway towards the party. "*Uh,*" I gasped as I was yanked into one of the guest rooms.

CHAPTER 17

Muffled

The door shut behind me. His hand pressed against it. Chase stroked my cheek. "It took you long enough to find me," he said.

"I told you to grab some air. Not play hide and seek."

"What is it the old people say? Those who seek shall find. Here I am." He held his arms wide.

He pecked me on the lips. I didn't respond. His fingers tickled my chin, flashing me a seductive smile. "Are you mad at me?"

"Not mad. Confused. Where is the gentleman I met and spent time with on the balcony? He's been missing since I told you about that dream."

"Is this about the remark I made?" He whispered, licking his lips.

"Yes." I looked away.

"I'm sorry," he said. He turned my face back towards him. I lifted my eyes to look into his. "I'll explain later. Let me make it up to you."

He raised my dress and ran his hands across my thighs gently. As he slid down my torso, he grabbed my panties with his teeth and pulled them to the floor. "You still want the morning treatment?" He asked, looking up at me like a sad, hungry puppy. I shook my head yes.

Sensually he licked, kissed, and flicked my vertical smile against the door. I sighed in silence as he fucked me with his tongue, trickling in his mouth as the vibration of his tongue inside me had me crawling up the back of the door.

"Is this what you wanted?" He murmured.

"Yes, but at your place." I sighed.

His oral highness picked up its pace. His fingers stepped in for action, competing with his tongue for insertion. My hands rested on his head, holding him in place against my clit, climaxing above his crown. He reached up and locked the door, then carried me into the walk-in closet. "The morning treatment is over," he said.

I panted out of breath, watching him move fast like a madman. He dragged the footstool near the bed inside the closet and sat on it. "Come here," he commanded. I obeyed. He *ruched* my dress to my waist and nibbled on my lower abdomen. "Now turn around."

I rotated my body to face the custom shoe rack newly installed. My ass jiggled from the soft bites gnawing on my cheeks. "Bend over." I did as commanded. "We're about to play *Can The Neighbors Hear Me Scream*," he said. I pivoted my torso to stand straight, but Chase bent me back towards the rack by my waist. *Smack!* His hand landed on my ass. I jolted forward and reached for the bottom shelf of the rack. "Spread those legs so I can see that pussy jump for me." His hands coached my thighs to open wider. "Pretty cunt," he moaned.

The wetness of his tongue mixed with my wet folds. Sturdy strong licks wavered on my tunnel. I gasped for air as an unexpected second smack landed on my bum hard enough to leave a print. My breathing increased rapidly and I jittered in my stance. "That's right. You're being punished," he said. *Smack! Smack!* His palms hard-pressed into my ass. "First you keep this good pussy from me all week. Then I find you talking to the man you wanted me to share you with." He muttered. *Smack!*

"What?" I muffled under my fist.

"This pussy likes to be punished I see. Look at her throb for me. Did my little bad girl miss this cock?"

"Mmm hmm." I moaned.

Chase rose to his feet and entered my drenched walls, grunting loudly to be heard by the neighborhood. The music and laughter from the other room drowned him out, so he oscillated furious jabs in my pussy. I held my fist in my mouth to win the game. The curve of his dick hit me in spots with such force, I wanted to scream "*Stop!*" But also shout "*Fuck me you psychopath!*" because it felt so good. I didn't want him to stop. I wanted him to keep going. Keep punishing me. Keep making my kitty purr for him.

"I told you this pussy was mine. Look at how *you* taking this dick. Let the neighbors hear you call my name." He smacked my ass again.

I didn't cave. I took the beating until the end. Determined to win the game. And focused on my line of questioning once he came. Heavy slaps painfully orchestrated with the pillage of his rough curved cock echoed between the walls. "Ah," I expelled, one after the other, careful not to scream unlike his boisterous finale inside of me.

He held my ass so close to him, our skin peeled apart when he finally released me from his clutch. I turned to him. "You must want the neighbors to hear you scream." I rolled my eyes.

"I want the neighbors to know you're mine." He panted.

"What did you mean you found me talking to the man I wanted you to share me with?" I shoved him aside and grabbed a towel from the drawer.

"I know everything. I told you to fix your shit. I didn't say go and actually fuck two men." He said reaching for me to hurry up with the towel.

"May I ask where you got this information?" I tossed him the cloth.

"One of your lovers congratulated me outside. He said I won the prize and told me about your secret meeting. Don't worry. I roughed him up a bit. Then he changed his tune and said he thought I should know he was respectfully walking away, but the other guy inside is who I needed to be worried about."

"And instead of asking me about this, you chose to run with words from a stranger, assume the person I was speaking to when you walked in had my affection, and then "punish" me for it by fucking me sideways in a house full of people?"

"You liked it. I could tell. That pretty little tight pussy is probably still aching for more."

It was.

I didn't dignify him with a response. I stood holding myself in the middle of the floor, watching him grin to himself. Proud of his performance. Proud he seduced me to do what he wanted, when he wanted.

He threw the towel inside the closet and closed the door. His grin vanished and a seriousness covered his face as he walked over to me. Wrapping his arms around me he said, "You did a nice job with this house. I see why that guy wants to hire you. But Miami is out of the question."

My eyes tightened and head swayed back. He held me tighter in his arms, confining me to his grasp.

"Do me a favor," I said.

"Anything for you."

"Wait in here for a couple of minutes after I leave. I don't want to embarrass my uncle. Okay?"

"What if I hang in the lounge room and watch television. I'm done mingling with this pretentious crowd."

"Sure. You go ahead."

I breathed out an abundance of emotions when he exited the room, and threw myself on the bed. While staring at the ceiling, I grew frustrated with myself. The man who had me balled up in a knot on the bed, had my shmoonda gyrating, and healing as his red flags flew with fire blazing from them. *But my goodness that maniac could fuck.*

Miami was looking pretty good in that moment. I plotted how I could begin again, work my way around Mr. Coppin's circle, and be more careful of the strangers I picked up. Even though none of them would compare to Rich Daddy Donovan. I was certain about one thing as I lied there in distress.

I have to get rid of Chase Alonso.

CHAPTER 18

Lisa

Quietly I eased out of the bedroom and rejoined the party. Chase eventually emerged from the den and latched on to my hip, tugging and repeatedly whispering in my ear, "I'm ready to go home." Uncle Jeff watched us closely. I squirmed and frowned when I knew he was looking. Laughed with a minor ripple from my throat, and chewed on my nails.

I stalled until the house emptied and the food wound down to scraps. I grabbed garbage bags from the pantry and Uncle Jeff turned off the music. "Here you go," I said. Chase's eyes narrowed at me.

Uncle Jeff witnessed his glare, walked over to me and squeezed my cheeks. "Job well done Amber. Everyone loves what you've done with the house. Mr. Coppin wants to meet with you first thing in the morning. I'll clean this up. You say good night to your friend." He winked his eye at me.

The anger in Chase's face frightened me. He gave Uncle Jeff a deathly stare while his back was turned to him. "You have a good night Chase," said Uncle Jeff.

"You do the same. Sir." His voice cracked.

I warmed my arms with my hands as we stood near his car. "Are you a little girl or something?" He sucked his teeth and leaned against the driver's door.

"What?" I tightened my eyes.

"I've been waiting on you all night. Why didn't you tell him you were leaving with me?" He fiddled with his keys and blew out of his mouth.

"You were here to celebrate my accomplishment tonight, but you've complained the whole time. It's almost three o'clock in the morning and you heard him say I have a meeting in a few hours. Why are you being like this?" I shivered and rocked back and forth rubbing up and down on my arms.

"You and I had plans." He pointed at me.

"Yes. To be here tonight. Chase, I don't know what's going on with you, but I'm *gonna* say goodnight and go help my uncle clean up. I'll call you tomorrow." I backed away.

"No kiss?" He scoffed.

I continued walking towards the house, skipping over the cracks in the cement. "Amber!" he shouted. I turned around and gestured he lower his voice, then raised my palms to face the sky.

"What?" I whispered.

"I said—No kiss." He strolled across the street and grabbed me close. "Don't walk away from me when I'm talking to you. Now give me my kiss."

He stuck his tongue down my throat and squeezed my ass tight. I jittered and he stopped. "What's wrong?" He asked.

"I'm a little sore there."

He grinned. "I'll kiss it when I see you tomorrow."

"Good night." I pecked his lips and scurried in the house.

Uncle Jeff stood near the stairwell as I locked the door. "I've changed my mind about that one," he said.

"I'm leaning in the same direction as you." I raised my brow.

"Jeckyll and Hyde that one. I wish things worked out with you and Derrick. He's a nice boy working his way up in his father's firm."

"Uncle Jeff, I... I think you should know Derrick is not my type. It was never going to happen." My voice deepened.

"I won't bring it up again," he said.

I went into the pantry and grabbed a can of wipes from the kitchen, then returned to the foyer, wiping the handprints from the glass table and vase at the foot of the stairs. Uncle Jeff stood against the wall and scratched his head. "I guess I'm no matchmaker. But I do prefer him over that smug faced prick who just left here."

"He is a prick. Isn't he?"

We shared a high five and laughed together. "You go on to bed and get ready for your big meeting tomorrow. I'll have a service come in and make this place spic and span," he said.

"Thanks. Good night." I saluted him like a soldier.

The long, hot shower nearly burned my skin and didn't help me wind down, or turn down the volume in my mind. It was quiet in the house, yet all I heard was noise inside my head. *What do I say tomorrow? What do I wear tomorrow? How crazy is Chase? When is Rich going to step up?*

I tossed and turned as the clock ticked above my head, then sat on the edge of the bed: restless, nervous, and anxious. With my heart racing, I looked up and saw it was 5 a.m. I grabbed the blanket at the foot of the bed and wrapped it around me. Out on the balcony I stood as the cold breeze froze my face. Pieces of my hair tickled my lips. I closed my eyes and inhaled the freshness of the morning saltwater.

When I opened them, there he was, running down the stretch while the waves pushed forward. I leaned against the rail in the darkness and watched as his silhouette grew closer. He strode past the house, ignorant he had a voyeur.

As he approached the house next door, he turned his body around and ran in place. I stood still as a mime, blending in with the darkness. He stared, still running in place, still stealing my heart.

I waited for him to continue his path, then returned to the warmth of my bed, and snuggled under the covers with a smile on my face. Our short exchange at the bar crossed my mind. I laughed internally and the pressure from my chest alleviated. Finally. Rest.

PERFECT TIME to break out the expensive heels I bought on Uncle Jeff's credit card in Beverly Hills. With my hair pulled back in a bun, a crisp white buttoned blouse, and black A-line skirt, I walked into Mr. Coppin's office on the ground floor of his house, the biggest on the strip by far.

His secretary, a local looker with high boobs who lucked up with high pay. "Mr. Coppin will see you know." Her red lips announced barely cracking a smile.

"Thank you." I walked passed her with my head held high.

She followed me inside and closed the door as Mr. Coppin stood from behind his desk and held his phone to his chest. "Amber. Come. Have a seat." I pulled out the antique wooden chair and sat across from him. *These will be upgraded with pillows.*

Mr. Coppin held up his finger and mouthed, "One sec." I observed the theme of his office and quickly figured it out. *Old rich man.* He hung up the phone, "I'm glad we could have this meeting before I fly down south in a few days. We have a lot to discuss. First things first." He slid a prewritten check for fifty thousand dollars across the desk. "This is a deposit for your services. Jeff said he paid you 35K. I'll pay you more as my house is bigger. My properties in Florida will pay significantly more. The only preference I have is to make my house modern and tasteful."

"Ugh, I brought color schemes and examples of some looks for you to choose from." I opened my folder on his desk.

"Not necessary. From what I saw of your uncle's place, I trust your judgement." He slid an envelope towards me. "Open it."

Inside was a single ticket for a charity banquet later that evening. "Can you make it?" He asked.

"I'm sorry. I don't understand. Am I decorating this place?"

"Certainly not." He chuckled. "I trust a girl like you knows how to dress for a black-tie affair among the elite?" He clicked his tongue.

"Y-Yes." I stammered.

"Of course you do. I'll send a car. See you tonight?" He pressed a button and his secretary opened the door.

"Tonight. Right." I flapped the envelope and followed her out.

CHAPTER 19

The Chopping Block

I left Mr. Coppin's house and crossed my fingers I would find an elegant black dress at The Oaks Shopping Center. *Black should be an easy find.* Incessant ignored calls from Chase, and a few hours of traffic and shopping had my heart fluttering down to the wire before the car arrived.

Frequently, I smoothed the sides of my slicked back hair hanging down on the side afraid of frizz. Plopping my matte lips, I checked my messages during the chauffeured drive into the city.

Chase: *I haven't heard from you. Call me.*

Chase: *Whatever I did I'm sorry. Waiting to hear from you.*

Chase: *If you don't call me back. Fuck it. I'm coming over.*

Rich: *I...I... was thinking of you. Talk to you soon.*

Mom: *Did that professor ever get in contact with you? You never called me back. You know I hate when you don't call me back.*

Chase: *Just tell me what I need to do so I can see you. Please. I'm sorry.*

I silenced my phone and tossed it inside my black velvet

clutch. "We've arrived ma'am," said the chauffeur. The car stopped and he opened my door, escorting me out by hand. I strutted down the red carpet, overly confident and curious of the people I was about to subject myself to.

If beauty were a competition, I was a contestant inside the banquet. Pretty women, young and old owned the room. Designer gowns, red lips, and four-inch heels. Regal, wealthy men at their sides. Some handsome, some just rich.

Elegant table top settings of dried roses, candlelight, name cards, and centerpieces I memorized to recreate later, eluded to the ceremonial ambiance of the room. I was around money. And I was alone.

I took a deep breath and grabbed a glass of champagne offered by the staff. Above the rim of the glass I searched for Mr. Coppin. There was no sign of him, but a slew of men I wouldn't mind spending ten minutes alone with in the bathroom stalls. The lights flickered like at the opera, "Ladies and Gentlemen, please take your seats. We will begin momentarily," said the emcee.

"May I escort you to your seat madam?" A host asked.

"Thank you."

"Your ticket please."

I handed him the envelope.

"Right this way."

I was led to a table up front with mostly empty chairs, one couple, and two men. I nodded and smiled, searching for Mr. Coppin once again. "Nice dress." Said one of the men.

"Thank you." I smiled.

"That shade of red fits you honey. Not everyone knows how to pull off a blue red." Said the man sitting beside him.

"It's all in the liner." I winked at him.

"You must know someone pretty major sitting at this table. I'm Kal by the way. This is my partner Miles."

"I came here at the last minute as a seat filler it seems. Mr. Coppin is my boss."

Kal and Miles gasped and shared a look with each other, then gave me a look of approval and envy. "You're rolling with the big dogs honey."

The couple at the other end of the table rolled their necks back and forth during my exchange with the gossip and makeup critics. The lights dimmed and music switched from elevator music to an orchestra selection. The host walked onto the stage. "I guess we better hush now," said Kal.

"Nice talking with you." I whispered.

As the host welcomed the guests and reviewed the strides of the charity over the years, I finally laid eyes on Mr. Coppin, sitting on the stage alongside the other founders of the charity. Staring into my direction. I broke his gaze and my eyes wandered the room, capturing the gaze of another, and another, and another. Men and women. Either I had fresh meat written on my forehead, or sitting at Mr. Coppin's table put me on the chopping block. *I hope this isn't some sort of 'Eyes Wide Shut' party.*

One by one each founder spoke, earning a few laughs from the audience before a list of items the guests bid on were brought to the stage. During the excitement of winners being announced, the host who escorted me to my seat returned with a drink and a note.

I had no idea you'd be here tonight. Check your messages. ~R.

I placed the note inside my purse and turned on my phone. It lit with messages from Chase, Rich, and Uncle Jeff.

Chase: *Come outside.*

Uncle Jeff: *The crazy guy is parked outside. Is everything okay?*

Rich: *I love your hair like that. What do you say we blow this joint and make a night of it?*

Chase: *I'll be here until you come home.*

I replied to Chase first.

'Sorry I missed you. Something came up. I don't know how long I will be tonight. Call you tomorrow.'

I sighed after responding to him. Something about his psycho sex still had me considering him, when I knew good dick wasn't worth all of the drama he was bringing to the table.

Second, I diffused the situation and alerted my uncle the Chase problem was taken care of. I exhaled with hopes Chase went home. Lastly, I responded to Rich.

'You never took me out on that date. You never said those three words. The last time was the last time. Muah'

The auction finalized with a standing ovation of having met their goal and the party began. Drunk and happy patrons took to the dance floor, cliques gathered in circles, and Mr. Coppin finally made his way over to me. "I knew you would be a showstopper," he said.

"This old thing." I blushed.

"How about you and me hit the dance floor?"

"Sure. Why not?"

He took me by the hand and led me to the center of the floor. A midtempo song didn't require the closeness of his body on mine, but I played along, giggling and raising his hands off of my ass. *What the fuck is happening here?*

"I asked you here tonight for a reason," he said.

"Oh?" I pretended it wasn't obvious.

"I have a proposition to make you a very rich woman, and change your life." His hands went back down to my ass.

"How so?" I raised them again.

Rich tapped him on the shoulder, "May I cut in Coppin?"

Mr. Coppin gritted his teeth.

"We're actually in the middle of discussing something Donovan."

"One dance?" Rich raised his brows and placed his hands in the small of my back.

Did I melt in front of everyone?

Mr. Coppin placed my hand inside Rich's. "One dance," he said. Rich nodded. "We'll finish this at the table." He said squeezing my shoulder, then rolled his eyes at Rich.

"What game are you playing?" I asked Rich.

"I'm not playing a game. I'm biding my time. That doesn't mean I have to suffer and watch you dance with that old crow." Rich sucked his teeth.

"That old crow just hired me this morning. I can make a lot of money working for him."

"Trust me when I say, he has more in mind than the work you're thinking of. Enough about him. Let's get out of here. I have to have you tonight."

"Why not every night?"

"Soon enough." His fingers hung close to the dip above my ass.

I didn't remove them. He moaned.

"I won't wait for you Rich."

"I didn't ask you to. Just like I didn't ask that tight little pussy to jump for me just now."

I scoffed under my breath. "You still haven't said it you know."

"I did say it." His voice deepened.

"During a blowjob doesn't count. Say it to my face. Right here. Right now." I gazed into his eyes.

"I love you Amber."

I beamed and held back kissing him in front of everyone. Rich gazed into my eyes and licked the corner of his mouth. "You would say it in front of a bunch of strangers when I can't jump your bones and have my way with you." I smiled.

"There's plenty of hotels nearby. We can still get out of

here to celebrate and make a night of it. How did you get here?"

"Mr. Coppin ordered me a car." I turned towards the table and flinched at the many eyes watching us. "Why didn't you tell me everyone is looking at us."

"Fuck them. I'm parked out front. Send me a message when you've ditched your boss."

He curtsied and let go of my hand. I walked off of the dance floor and joined Mr. Coppin at the table. He introduced me as his date to the now filled seats. Kal and Miles pursed their lips and clapped on their sides for me to see. I shook my head and laughed internally.

"If you'll excuse us," Coppin said.

He pulled out a chair at the empty table next to the one we were assigned. I sighed lowly, anxious to meet up with Rich, and not in the mood for the shenanigans about to cause me to lose out on making money designing his homes. *The fuckery.*

"Before we were so rudely interrupted, I was about to share with you the opportunity of a lifetime."

"So, you said." I smiled with my mouth closed.

"I need a wife. A wife like you who turns heads when she enters a room. A man of my status gets off on that sort of thing. Now, I know I'm older than you like them."

I cut him short. "What does that mean?"

"I know about you and Rich. I saw you two out on the rocks. And again, at the party. Imagine my shock when I heard you in the bedroom with that young fella. I can't say I blame him. I'm here right now begging to be him."

"Mr. Coppin I..."

"Wait. Wait. Allow me to finish. None of what I'm saying is to offend you. I'm proposing your hand in marriage. An open marriage with a few restrictions. You'll have a monthly allowance and live a life of luxury. I only require you attend all functions I request and make me look good."

"What are the restrictions?" I looked up at him dismayed.

"Be discreet with your lovers in public, sleep with me once every season, and under no circumstances are you to continue seeing Rich Donovan."

CHAPTER 20

Papers

The waiter sat two champagne flutes on the table in front of us. Mr. Coppin handed me a glass and held his forward. "To us." He toasted with a grin written across his lips.

"Come again?" My brows furrowed and face dropped. "Why would I be restricted from seeing Rich?"

"Because I hate the bastard. He's not worth your time. He's a pretty boy who got lucky with a start-up living amongst people whom he doesn't belong." Mr. Coppin spoke vehemently.

"Those words can apply to my uncle, as well as myself," I said.

"But everyone loves Jeff. And soon you. Say yes and all of this can be yours." He squeezed my thigh. "Richie boy can only give you Malibu. I can give you the world." He attempted to *smize*, but failed. I know firsthand he'll disappoint you Amber."

"Can I have some time to think about it?" I sighed, then placed the glass on the table.

"My jet leaves for Florida on Wednesday. I hope you're on it."

I excused myself to the powder room. The stares I received were more than uninviting, and the sudden silence when I walked in announced loud and clear I was the hot topic.

I posed in front of an empty mirror hanging on the wall and adjusted my dress. The women glared at me behind my back. I reapplied my lipstick and blotted the residue on the papers I stashed in my purse. "You're definitely the newbie everyone's been whispering about." A woman wearing loud perfume and a dress my mother would wear said from the sink. The lounge grew quiet when I walked in, but after she spoke the silence was deafening.

"I beg your pardon?" I asked.

"Yeah, they're all in here gossiping about you. Wondering who you are and where you came from."

"Who is they?" I snapped my purse shut.

"The whole damn party."

I scoffed. "I doubt that."

"They're all wondering how you're sitting at Cop's table, then danced with his known enemy."

"I'm here as a seat filler ma'am. I don't know anything about these people. You have a good night." I stepped towards the door.

The woman placed her clutch in front of me. "You be careful. I was the first casualty of that war. Don't be the second. And whatever *Cop* offers you—get it in writing." Her voice shook.

The red in the corner of her eyes startled me, but the puffiness in her dark circles led me to believe she was either sad, or had worried too much. "I didn't catch your name," I said.

"I'm you twenty years ago. The second Mrs. Coppin.

Here's some advice my mother got wrong. Marry for money the first time. Marry for love the second. You won't always look the way you do tonight." She lowered her purse.

"Nice meeting you." I nodded.

Back inside the ball, Mr. Coppin was laughing loudly with his jacket off and the top of his shirt unbuttoned at our assigned table. Rich stood off in the corner with a group of gentlemen eyeing a young blonde filly who had too much to drink. I changed my direction and stood outside under the loading zone.

My chauffeur of the evening rolled the car around. I tapped on the window and asked, "Do I have you for the entire evening?"

"I'm yours until I'm dismissed madam."

"Give me your number. I may need you to pick me up in the morning. Will that be okay?"

"Yes." He tipped his hat and slipped his card between my fingers.

I returned to the walkway and called Chase. One ring and he answered. "How fast can you get to the Beverly Wilshire?" I snickered.

"On my way," he said.

"Text when you arrive."

To kill time, I wandered the empty halls of the hotel. I studied the painting selections up and down the banquet hall until they bored me. As I turned down the hall of the banquet, I ran into Kal and Miles. "Honey you better get back in there. Your Daddy Warbucks is looking for you." Kal said pulling on his lapel. I twirled my eyes.

"And you said you were a seat filler. The man is bragging to everyone how you're his date for the evening. Lock that old money down honey. Viagra may be his friend tonight, but that diet of his is yours." Miles winked and snapped his fingers.

"I guess I better get back in there, huh. Talk to you two later." I slid between them.

I returned to our table with a fresh glass of champagne, laughing at unfunny jokes and waiting for my phone to buzz. The amount of bragging from Mr. Coppin and his elite friends made my stomach turn. I kept my glass to my lips to keep from frowning.

Finally, my purse vibrated in my lap.

RICH: *What's the hold up? Are you starting to fall for the old crow?*

WHAT'S WRONG? **:ME**

THE DRUNK BLONDE WENT HOME WITH SOMEONE ELSE?

RICH: *???*

COPPIN PLACED his hand on my thigh and I swallowed air. My back stiffened and my legs locked. He leaned closer, "You were gone quite a while."

"Yes, I got into some girl talk in the powder room. You know how we girls love to gab." I sighed.

"I wasn't the only one looking for you. Remember what I said about him." He squeezed my thigh. "Have you thought about my offer, or were you serious about needing time to think it over?"

"How soon can you have the papers drawn up?" My legs shivered.

"We can leave now and go somewhere to discuss it."

A chill traveled through my body. "This champagne is running right through me. If you'll excuse me. I need to visit the ladies again."

"Are you sure you girls aren't partying in there?" He hummed with laughter.

"I'll never tell."

I exited the hotel through the revolving door. The wind picked up significantly within the hour, and my hair blew wildly away from my face. I coughed from the smell of tobacco cutting my breath in the breeze. "I apologize. I wouldn't have sparked my cigar had I known I'd be in the presence of a lady." Said a gentleman I gave a once over lurking about inside the party.

"I'll be out of your hair in a minute," I said.

"No. Please don't. I'd love the company." He pressed the cigar against the bricks and blew smoke behind him. "It's pretty intense in there. Isn't it?"

"That would be an understatement." I stepped into the drop zone.

The chauffeur pulled in front of me and lowered the window. "Shall I escort you home madam?" I shook my head side to side.

"I should be leaving here shortly." I checked the time on my phone. "I'll wave goodbye and you can take off for tonight. I'll call you if I need you."

He signaled *ten-four* then shifted his eyes to the guy putting out the cigar. I stepped back on the pavement. "You must be a big deal, having your very own personal driver. Should I know you?" His eyes followed my curves. I pressed my lips together and turned away. "Seriously, are you the next big thing out here?"

"No. I'm not. But thank you for the compliment." I blushed, looking over my shoulder.

"You seem like the next big thing in there."

"I didn't see you inside." I sassed him.

"But I saw you."

I laughed. "You need to work on your pick-up lines."

He laughed. "That would have worked back in my day."

"I'm sure it would have."

A revving engine cut the corner and turned into the lot.

The hairs on my arms stood up, and I broke my laugh with the gentleman. "Well nice chatting with you." I walked into the drop off zone.

"Very nice. I didn't catch your name," he said.

"It's not important." I replied, watching my Latin Lover drive like a madman in the lot.

"It is to me. I'm Phillip."

Chase drove up in his '69 GTX. I waved to the chauffeur and he flashed his lights. With a huge smile on his face, Chase leaned over and shouted through the window, "There's my girl! Get in here you foxy ass..."

"Hold on there, son." Phillip cut him short.

"What?" Chase's face wrinkled. "Son? Who are you?"

Phillip bravely walked over and opened the car door. He placed his hand in the center of my back and delicately slid his fingers down to the small dip above the groove of my buttocks. "The name's Phillip Gary. And you son, you should be opening doors for this beautiful, young woman." He kissed the back of my hand.

"Nice meeting you Phillip." My cheeks turned rosier than the blush I powdered with.

He closed the car door and we shared a smile until Chase revved the engine. "Who the fuck is that guy?"

I shrugged. "You heard him. He said his name is Phillip."

"You and these ritzy assholes." He shook his head and sucked his teeth. "I'm glad I'm out of the dog house. Where do you want to go?"

"Just drive." I said, looking at Phillip from the side view mirror.

CHAPTER 21

Salty

"You missed me, huh." Chase's face glowed as we passed under the street lights. His energy filled the car. He truly was over the moon I called him. And as crazy and possessive as he was, I breathed for the first time when he rescued me from the chaos.

"Yeah, I missed you," I placed my hands on the back of his head and ran my fingers through his tapered cut.

"I hope you don't have any plans tomorrow."

"What if I do?"

"Then you're fucked. I already told my crew they won't see me tomorrow. Consider yourself kidnapped. Look behind you."

I shook my head while thinking to myself, *'This possessive bastard really is crazy about me.'*

I turned around in my seat and reached for the bags, and two boxes behind me. A dozen fuchsia roses placed inside a Glam Fleur box brought a smile to my face. "I've never seen roses this color or with such flair," I said.

"Read the card."

Thank God you called me before these died.
Now let me taste your lips.

I pinched his arm and leaned towards him. Chase held onto my thigh and pecked my lips with his eyes on the road. "I'm sorry I stayed away for so long. I needed some time to myself." I put a red kiss on his cheek.

"We're together now. That's all that matters. I'll spoil what's in the bags. I bought us matching pajamas. Corny I know. But now you have something to walk around the house in."

Damn. He is serious about me staying with him.

"Thank you. You're so sweet."

"Now open the other box," he commanded.

I untied the gold ribbon and lifted the lid. "Put them on." He smiled showing his teeth. I removed my linear drops and screwed the diamond studs into my ear. "You like?"

"I love," I said. "How mu..What made...Thank you. They're perfect."

"Anything for you babe."

My phone buzzed in my pursed.

RICH: *I'm ready to leave this bore fest. Where are you?*

I've left. We need to talk. I'll call you. : **ME**

Covering my bases, I sent a message to Uncle Jeff, *Don't wait up,* then sent a text to myself before silencing my phone. *Phillip Gary.*

Music and light conversation passed the time as missed the exit to Malibu and Cornell. "I'm a man of my word. We're spending the night in Santa Barbara."

I blushed and tightened my shoulders, then removed my shoes for the hour drive ahead. Observing the night scenery along the coast was just as beautiful as it was in the day. It could have been the moment. It could have been the clear night sky. Either or, the views were breathtaking all the way to the hotel sitting on the beach.

I sat in the car while Chase checked in. He returned and grabbed a blanket from the trunk, then led me through the side gate of the hotel. I wrapped the blanket around me and followed him to the pool area where he grabbed a chair and carried it down to the beach near the waves. "You *wanna* get wet now or later," he grinned and tapped on his lap.

I sat between his legs and covered us with the blanket. The ocean roared and the stars lit the navy sky like tiny diamonds in my ears. "I love it here. I don't know why. I just do."

"Is that the only thing you love?" He kissed the side of my face.

"Chase?"

"It's too soon. I know. But I've fallen for you Amber. I'm jealous and I love hard."

"I'd be lying if I didn't say I feel something for you too." I cut him short. "I want to tell you something, but with the way you've been acting lately…"

"I'm sorry. I get a little crazy when I feel threatened. And I felt threatened at that party."

"So is the person I'm talking to right now the crazy, jealous guy, or the guy I shared laughs with on the balcony?"

Chase laughed. "Are you purposefully talking so I don't say it?"

"You should hear what I have to say first. But not now. Let's enjoy this moment and this view tonight."

He snuggled me close and I stared at the luminescent waves crash near my feet. The breeze grew stronger and the tide nearer to the surface. I warmed my hands beneath his under the blanket. "How do you feel about marriage?" I asked.

He choked on his words and coughed. "Why? You *wanna* marry me?"

"Just answer the question. Are you the marrying kind?"

"I would marry you." He held me tight. "Does this have to do with you staying in the apartment?" He kissed the back of my head.

"It's not a loaded question Chase. And let's be honest. We both know that apartment would be a storage for my things if I moved in."

"If?" His chest pounded against my back. "Why are you still on the fence about staying?"

"I've upset you. I didn't mean to," I said.

I didn't need to face him to know the vein on the side of his neck was plump. I acted fast and placed my hand on his cock. "You deserve a little something for being my hero tonight and bringing me all the way out here," I said.

The smile on his face disappeared and he adjusted himself against my back. His lips parted open and kissed me. I released his pretty, curved penis and he exhaled. "I've been wanting you to touch me since you hopped in my car." His dick twitched and chest pounded beneath his shirt.

I tucked the blanket behind him in the chair and placed my knees in the wet sand. The cold air erected Chase's cock harder than the shells pressed against my toes. I dove my head full throttle on his dick and slicked it. I came up for air and stroked it with both hands. His head leaned back and he sighed. I rolled my tongue across his tip while I stroked him, feeling my wetness trickle down and drenching in my panties. I moaned from the urgency growing in me to be fucked. And only the way he could fuck me.

The cold was no match for the heat growing inside him. Both sets of my lips were soaked, and to my delight, Chase took his hand and lifted my dress until his fingers could play with my pussy. "Sucking this dick turns you on. I like that," he moaned.

I looked up at him and our eyes met. The waves traveled further inland, dampening my legs as I trembled from the fingering and frigid temperature of the water. Chase looked ahead at the open darkness. "I won't let the ocean swallow you," he said.

"Allow me to swallow you."

I smirked and sucked him hard and long until my neck ached and tongue needed a break, using the sexual tension I felt for Rich inside the banquet on him. I was soaked from the tide from my feet to my thighs. Water sprinkled on my lips as I fed on his cock slowly, tasting his salt and that of the ocean. He jerked from the sensitivity of my throat massaging his curve, and squeezed the base of his cock while holding my mouth hostage around his dick until he was relaxed and breathless.

I lifted my head and spat his cream into the wave receding from my knees, and wiped my mouth. Chase sat upright and gazed at me with calming eyes and a curve on the side of his lip. "I'm not going to let you leave me," he said. "I love you."

My eyes blinked fast and my mouth parted slightly. "Let's get you inside. You're freezing." He said, now towering over me.

In that moment, I accepted I would never be free of Chase Alonso. Now it was up to him to accept he would never have me all to himself.

CHAPTER 22

Paperchaser

The look on Uncle Jeff's face cut me like a knife when I walked in Monday night wearing pajamas for my walk of shame. "That boy didn't have the decency to walk you to the door," he said. I hid my face and continued up the stairs, listening to him lecture me.

I acknowledged my mistakes then apologized. "It won't happen again." I said like a chastised teenager, then smirked with my back turned to him.

"Mr. Coppin came by looking for you. He said he called you all morning. I tried to reach you as well. What's gotten into you? I thought you were ready to jump start your career?"

"By chance did your friend Mr. Coppin tell you why he stopped by?"

"No. But as a high paying client, he's going to expect you to answer your phone when he calls."

"You're right. My mistake. I'll go call him right now."

I lied. I powered on my phone and did an online search of Phillip Gary. Message after message chimed while I searched for his profile. "Hot damn," I said to myself. Mr. Phillip Gary had a common name, but won the popularity contest due to his profession as a lawyer and upbringing. Son of a Former Ms. World Competitor and Hollywood Studio Founder, Mr. Gary was sure to be an ace in my pocket.

I searched his name on dating sites and came up empty. Then searched for him on social media. One profile with no recent activity. I double tapped his last post as bait. *If he responds it was meant to be. Now damage control.*

A short stroll fifteen minutes later, Coppin welcomed me inside his home. "You disappeared last night," he said.

"I had plans prior to your invite." I lied. "One day I'll feel comfortable saying no instead of spreading myself thin."

"I see. Does this visit mean you've made a decision?" He probed.

"Pardon me for assuming you had the papers drawn. I was told you came by the house." *I'm regretting this already. He's trying to hustle me.* "May I see them?"

"I was surprised to see the check hadn't been deposited this morning."

"I'm here to discuss that as well."

"I'd prefer to avoid the five-day hold. Can you transfer it into my account?"

He grinned on the side of his mouth and dialed his accountant. "Hello Claire, Transfer 200K into the account of Amber Edmonds asap. I'll have her forward her information over tonight. Yeah. Call me when it's taken care of." He passed me a yellow envelope.

What game is he running?

I opened the envelope and skimmed through the agreement. "Are any of these terms negotiable?"

"Such as?" He raised a brow.

"I'll return it tomorrow with my changes. Let's discuss then."

"There is something I need to amend myself."

"Which is?"

"Every once in a while, you'll look at me the way you look at him."

I choked on my rebuttal. "I'll see myself out."

I held the papers close to my chest on the walk home in deep conversation with myself.

*I'm not a hooker or a high-priced call girl pretending to be in love for an hour. I simply fuck who I want. Always for desire. Never for pay. But this arrangement will change all of that. What I came out here to achieve is happening as if the devil was listening to my thoughts and granting me my wish with a side of sacrifice your soul. Humph. Two I love **yous** by handsome men, and one promise to give me the world by a man I had no attraction to. Love will have to wait.*

It was near midnight when Chase called. "Was coming back earlier than I planned worth it?" He said licking his lips through the screen.

"Of course I'm going to say no with you looking at me like that."

He had worked his magic on me once again in Santa Barbara.

"I was thinking I could swing by tomorrow after work. If that's cool." His biceps contracted in the frame.

"Are you doing what I think you're doing?" I giggled.

The camera traveled down his perfect abs for the money shot. His palms cupped his girth and massaged the hooked tip of his cock. "You know you want to be on it," he said.

"I have some things to handle in the morning. Come over. I'll sneak you inside."

"Don't tempt me. I'll come wake those ritzy assholes up." His eyes glinted in the camera.

"What if we play a different game this time. Loser has to share a secret."

"Be there in twenty minutes."

The notification on my phone chimed while I waited for Chase. *Phillip Gary sent you a message.* "Ooh," I murmured.

If you're up call me. Phil

He answered and I led. "I have about ten minutes. What's up?"

"You at this hour." He laughed.

"Your sense of humor is one of a kind." I joined him in laughter.

"I've been reimagining your face all day. The Gods must be on my side for I'm looking at those pretty brown eyes right now. You are stunning."

"Phillip, I've gotta say…"

He interrupted, "Please, call me Phil."

"Phil, I can't say I've met anyone who speaks like you. Has anyone ever told you that before?"

"Just you pretty lady. What are you doing up at this hour?"

"I'm a very blunt person Phil, you don't want to know the answer to that question." I placed my finger in my mouth.

"Try me." He smiled like a neighborhood gossip about to hear the latest rumor.

"I'm about to fuck my boyfriend." I giggled.

"Is he there with you right now?" He whispered.

"No. He'll be here in a few minutes." I rose from the bed and opened the blinds.

"Damn I wish I was him." He rose his brows. "Can I watch?"

"Phil, you're filthy." I purred. "I like it. But what's in it for me?"

"Whatever you want." His voice turned sultry.

"Hmmm. How about a meeting tomorrow morning?"

"I'd love to take you to breakfast."

"Deal. Put your phone on mute. He's here."

Phillip's face was flushed. I placed my phone between the stack of towels and t-shirts on the dresser. "Be right back." I whispered, then crept down the stairwell. I eased open the door and waved for Chase to come on. He strolled across the street effortlessly cool, and mauled me before both of his feet crossed the threshold. "Look at you. Sexy and smart driving the hybrid over here."

"You said we're playing the quiet game tonight, right?" He winked.

I pulled him inside and led the way to my room. His jacket dropped to the floor as I locked my door. "My dick's been hard for you all night. Come here," he said. His palms held my face against his. "You drive me crazy Chica."

"Remember the game. Whoever makes the most noise loses." I mumbled in between his tender kisses.

I lowered his grey sweats and stroked him 'til he sighed. He lifted my t-shirt and kissed me maniacally everywhere he pleased. My breasts filled his mouth before he lifted me in the air and spread me open for a taste. I swallowed my sigh holding on to air, lightly nervous I would gyrate and fall to the floor, mostly aroused at his strength and balance and creativity.

How the fuck am I going to give up this man?

With full control he held me open and steered his spear inside my pussy. I gulped on air as he bounced me up and down and side to side, using my ass in his hands as a guide. I panted lowly, biting his shoulders while coming to the sounds of his intense breathing burying his moans.

He sat me on the bed. I wiped his mouth with his shirt and kissed him, then placed my finger between his lips. "Don't make me wait for it," I whispered. My finger trailed down his chin past his chest, then along the curve of his cock. I offered my throat to it, willingly and generously. He held the back of my head, pressing the line of my hair against his inverted abdomen until I choked and he gurgled. With one finger under my chin, he lifted my face then smiled at me devilishly. "You're losing." I whispered.

My legs spread wide in the air, then cradled my head. Chase slicked my track line from south to north, then north to south with a hard tongue, then drilled two fingers in and out of my pussy, sneaking licks in between until I moaned beneath my covered mouth.

The surprising pressure of his pipe entered my center, storming my capital with deep broad strokes. His hands squeezed my ass posed in the air for the taking. He dug sideways in a corner and I gasped, constraining the vocal outburst on the tip of my tongue inside. He grinned wickedly, "Call that Chase's Corner," he whined. "Let that shit out. Don't hold back." He growled and teased, forcing my pussy to throb with each pivot. "I *wanna* hear you say it. Say you love me."

I observed his gorgeous face, his supple lips, and his tight eyes studying my mouth to remember how I looked when I finally said the words. "I love you." I mouthed quietly. His eyes untightened and the head of his cock circled the top of my cavity. I panted aloud. "I love you." I said, putting a curve on the side of his lip.

"Yo tambien te amo. Dulzura de mi vida. Eres mia." He passionately said gazing into my eyes.

My muffled cry was drowned out by the gurgling groans from his thickened throat. He was about to explode. I thrusted forward and held him hostage between my legs

when he paused his last jab. Chase's legs trembled and tight-
ened. "Amber," he called out and came, grunting above me.
He leaned his long body over mine, "You win again Princess.
See you tomorrow?" I nodded and he kissed me good night.

Once Chase was out of the house, I checked in with Phil.
"You made my eyes water young lady. I've had a good life, but
I wish I was in that bloke's shoes the past twenty minutes. You
love him?"

"I do, but it's complicated."

"How so?"

"I'll tell you at our meeting in a few hours." I exhaled.

"Can't wait. I'll send you the reservation details in the
morning. Counting the minutes until then."

CHAPTER 23

The Contender

Phillip Gary. New to me and already unforgettable. From his odd, funny way with words and fortyish good looks, he kept my attention and I liked him right away, which was unusual. Not because of his age, but because of his quirky personality and jokey mannerisms. It only took two conversations to realize he was a delight to talk to, and for whatever ambiguous reason, the only person I let watch me fuck.

Before he became my voyeur, I briefly thought about fucking him the night we met, but as usual, Chase erased the other men in my life with a few strokes. I met my new friend at a swanky restaurant filled with upscale patrons who didn't have to work, enjoying their pastries and lattes and frappes early in the day at tables covered with white linen, and their miniature puppies peaking from their purses.

Phil stood when I walked in and kissed me on the cheek. "I must have rehearsed a thousand lines to say to you this morning so you wouldn't find me corny," he said.

"And. What did you come up with?" I smiled and placed my purse and the envelope on the table.

"I thought about you all night. Excuse the bags under my eyes." He joked.

"You look handsome to me."

"You're too kind." He returned to his seat.

He stared at me with stars in his eyes and a blank face. I assumed he was still picturing last night. My nipples erected thinking of it myself, adding him in on the action. I tilted my head to the side, "Phil?"

"So," he broke his gaze, "To what do I owe the pleasure?"

"I'm in a bit of a time crunch, and in need of legal counsel on this document." I handed the papers to him over the complimentary bread.

He opened it and jerked at the contents on the first page and looked up at me. "And here I was thinking I had a shot."

"A shot?" I inquired.

"Yeah. I came here with hopes you would agree to go on a date with me, but I can't compete with Charles. His money is long and this is a major financial move for you if you abide by the rules set in this pre-nup."

"I'd like to make amendments. How fast can I get that done?"

"After what you did for me last night, pronto."

He retrieved a pen from the inside of his blazer, clicked the top of it, and looked up at me. "What changes shall we make?"

"Label this marriage an open marriage.

- I'm allowed to discreetly maintain relationships with other parties without interference or forfeit of this agreement. The request to remove Richard Donovan will be agreed upon out of respect for the union. If the plaintiff does not abide by the guided restriction, Charles M. Coppin serves the right to dissolve the marriage and pay the plaintiff one million dollars.

- An annual stipend of two million dollars is to be paid due to the plaintiff. The stipend will increase to five million dollars once the union exceeds ten years.
- In the event of an annulment within twelve months after the exchange of nuptials, a payoff agreement of three million dollars and a signed NDA regarding the dissolution of the marriage.
- No interruptions during scheduled separation periods. The exception: Medical emergency.
- If spouse remains exclusive in the marriage for one continuous year, a bonus of one million dollars is to be added to the annual two million dollars stipend.
- This contract is to be revisited after two years, where the plaintiff has the option to remain in the marriage. If the plaintiff chooses to dissolve after twenty-four months, Charles M. Coppin agrees to a one-time payout of five million dollars in addition to the annual stipend.
- In the event of death, all bank account balances belonging to Amber Edmonds are to be transferred equally to Alma Edmonds and Chase Alonso, one million dollars of any insurance policy claims to be paid to Jeffrey Edmonds.
- If death falls upon the plaintiff within one year of the marriage, the annual stipend is to be paid solely *to Alma Edmonds.*
- All health and medical decisions remain with Jeffrey Edmonds as Healthcare Power of Attorney and Personal Representative.

- All monies obtained by the plaintiff prior to marriage are not negotiable and remain solely as private property of the plaintiff.
- In the event of death of Charles M. Coppin, the plaintiff requests rights to property of the home of her choice, one vacation home, full payout of agreed specified amount in a living will, twenty million in savings, and twenty five percent of the financial balance of all accounts, before distribution of funds are allocated to ex-spouses and children.
- Changes to this agreement can be modified every ten years."

Phil took a deep breath and raised his brows. "Anything else Ms. Edmonds?"

"I'm taking you on as my lawyer. You tell me."

"I'm not sure you needed me. You appear to have it all covered."

"Well now that you know this will be an open marriage, keep hope alive for that date." I held up my fist. "After all, you will be hanging around as my lawyer." I winked.

"You are one incredible creature Amber Edmonds. The day I get to lay you across my desk might be the day I go on home to glory."

I covered my mouth and chuckled. "Phil, the things you say…" My chuckle turned into a full laugh. "Now, shall we order?"

As Phil and I enjoyed a sweet array of treats and rich beverages, Coppin's accountant verified the transfer of my funds. I left Phil an hour later following funny banter and a promise to have the new draft available before the end of the business day.

"What the fuck!" I said parking my uncle's car. I placed

my sunglasses on and sashayed over to Chase. "I thought we were on for tonight." I kissed him and wrapped myself in his arms before addressing Professor Kelte. "I thought we said goodbye weeks ago."

"Can we talk in private?" Professor Kelte asked.

"No." Chase answered.

"The Amber I know can speak for herself." Kelte stared at me.

"The Professor I know was big on playing by the rules. We've said goodbye twice now. Yet here you are. Did you stop by to apologize?"

"For what?" his voice rose.

"You lied. When we last spoke, I told you I was serious about Chase. You fed him some bullshit the night of my party and slid away like a snake. I thought we had an under-standing?"

"We did, but then I realized I'm still in love with you." Kelte looked at me with thoughtful eyes and licked his lips.

"Get the fuck out of here!" Chase fumed and balled his fist.

"And I don't trust this guy with you. You belong with me."

"Wrong. She belongs **to me**." Chase shoved Kelte.

I stood in front of Chase and restrained him with my palms against his chest. His heartbeat was so strong, it felt like drums beating in my hands. I moved them to his face and begged. "Go in the house and wait for me, okay?"

"I'm not leaving you out here with the likes of him." Chase said gripping my arms.

"What if all three of us go inside and talk this out. We're making a scene." I pled.

"There isn't anything to talk about." Chase said glaring into my eyes. "You!" he shouted to Kelte. "Get in your car and leave. Now!"

I buried my face of embarrassment and stormed into the

house. Chase followed me inside. Uncle Jeff stopped him at the door. "What's going on?"

"I wish I knew. I need to check on Amber." Chase replied.

Kelte knocked on the open door and asked, "May I come in?"

My shoulders sunk as I turned around on the stairwell to face the chaos following me inside. "You are relentless," I said to Kelte.

"Who is he?" Uncle Jeff asked.

"A friend from college." I answered.

"No one of importance." Chase added.

A knock sounded behind Kelte. All of our eyes shifted to the open door. "Is this a bad time?" Rich asked leaning inside.

"It appears so," said Uncle Jeff.

"Shall I cancel our tee time?" Rich asked. "I hope not, I have something important I'd like to discuss with you." Rich glanced in my direction.

"Fuck was that?" Chase asked Rich.

"He's the one I told you to worry about," said Kelte.

CHAPTER 24

The Shark

All eyes in the room shifted to my direction. "Him!" Chase pointed looking at me. His red eyes and pulsing temple caused my heart to ache. Kelte's sultry eyes and smirked lip caused my blood to boil. Uncle Jeff's narrowed stare and pouted lip caused the little girl in me to lower my head of shame, and Rich's wide, hungry eyes and puckered lips caused me to hide my face.

The men of my past, present, and future found their way to me, but far from the way I had dreamed. For a second, I imagined Uncle Jeff was still on his vacation, and pictured the three of us fucking in every room of the house for an entire weekend. Me spread wide eagle on the stairs properly positioned to handle all three of them at once. The thought caused my pussy to throb and I snapped out of the daydream to face the nightmare standing in front of me.

"I have appointments I need to tend to and can't deal with this right now. Uncle Jeff see everyone out," I said.

"Except for me." Chase spoke boldly.

"You, follow me." I said leading him into the den.

He pressed me against the wall and planted his lips hard

against mine. I slid my hands under his shirt, and ran my hands up and down his back. "Even after all of that my dick is still hard for you. You fucked that old guy, didn't you?" He grinned.

"You lost the bet last night. You owe me a secret."

Chase's cheeks turned blush, his posture wilted, and his mouth twisted open. "Uh boy—Okay—The way I inherited the apartment building is not something I'm proud of. Wasn't my finest hour, let me say that. But, ugh, I was actually sleeping with the owner, and she left it to me in her will."

"Why is that a secret?"

"Because she was a sixty-year-old woman. I was 24 screwing her brains out." He stepped away and blushed. "If you fucked that old guy at the door, you have no room to judge me."

"He's not sixty." I said riddled with guilt.

"So, you did fuck him." He laughed.

"Look, I have an important meeting in a little while. It's imperative I see you tonight."

"What's wrong Princess?"

I huffed and looked away. Tears formed in the corner of my eyes, my stomach turned, and my palms turned sweaty as he hovered over me and gazed into my eyes. "Just be here." I said.

"I will. See you after work. Now let me hear it."

"I love you." I said, holding his face with one hand and his chest with the other.

"I love you too."

The house cleared and I dressed for my meeting with Phillip and Coppin. Uncle Jeff stood in the doorway to my room. "I'm off to the golf course. Thought I should check on you. Is everything okay?"

"Yeah. Everything's fine."

"I'm a tad worried they aren't," he said.

"I promise you. I know what I'm doing."

"I just had three angry men in my living room. It would appear you **don't** know what you're doing." He folded his arms.

"Uncle Jeff, I love you like you were my own father. You'll be proud of me. You'll see. I'll be home sometime tonight. We can catch up then. Okay?"

He shook his head.

Phillip Gary knocked on the door as Uncle Jeff was headed out. "My God another one," said Uncle Jeff.

"I beg your pardon." Phillip's eyes wandered.

"Never mind my uncle. How are we looking?" I reached for the envelope.

"All of your demands are listed. I cleared my calendar so you'll have representation present."

"I knew I liked you." I said, reviewing the changes. "Let's go."

Uncle Jeff smiled at me. "Maybe I **don't** need to worry about you." He said, smiling on his way out of the door.

Mr. Coppin paced the floor with one hand in his pocket, and the other across his lips as his attorney and Phillip went back and forth until the amendments were signed off.

Coppin added:

The marriage must be consummated the night we exchange nuptials, or the contract becomes null and void.

I added:

A good faith deposit of five hundred thousand dollars of the first-year stipend will be deposited into the private account of Amber Edmonds promptly after consummation.

Coppin signaled for me to join him on the balcony while our attorneys enjoyed a drink in the lounge. I kept my eyes ahead on the red orb in the sky falling behind the navy line. "You're a shark. We're going to make a great team. Have you packed for Miami yet?"

"I will tonight. What time will the car pick me up?" I asked.

"Two o'clock tomorrow afternoon."

"I'll be ready."

Phillip drove me back to the house and wished me luck. I went inside, grabbed a blanket and fold-out chair from out back, and found myself a quiet spot on the beach. I wrapped the blanket around me completely, leaving a small opening so my eyes could watch the waves reset and retrieve, thinking to myself how I would be watching this scene a few doors down when I returned from Miami.

Chase returned and met me out by the water. I sat in his lap and nestled against him under the blanket. "You alright?" he asked.

"No." I confessed.

"I feel like you were holding something back earlier. Do you want to tell me now?" He kissed my face.

"No matter what happens, know you're the one I love."

"Look at me. Nothing is going to happen."

I rested my back against his chest and fell asleep in his arms, dreaming of us together in another life. Sitting in the sand watching the sun rise and set like we did in Santa Barbara. In the dream I would wake up to his lip service in the morning, as a routine after treating me like a porn star the night before. I envisioned him staring at me with that twinkle in his eyes whenever he sees me. The look of lust written on his face when we're alone. The fire in his spirit when he's near me.

The chill of the night air turned vicious. He woke me with

kisses and a strong hug, then carried me inside where we said goodbye. Chase, oblivious it was the final time we would look into each other's eyes.

I held him in my arms and sniffed the faded cologne on his shirt, and listened to his heart beat one last time, then kissed him like the first night we slept together.

Uncle Jeff stopped by my room while I packed my things. "Going somewhere?" He frowned.

"I am. I wouldn't leave without telling you goodbye."

"You sure about that? You've avoided me since the fiasco from earlier today. What was that?"

I sighed. "A disaster I never saw coming."

"Today at golf, Rich asked about you."

"He's too late. I'm in love with someone else. Besides, things will be different when I return."

"How so?"

I zipped my suitcase and stacked my duffle bag on top of it, then gave my uncle a hug. "Thank you for everything. Inviting me out here has changed my life. I don't know where I would be if it weren't for you."

"Is everything okay? Do I need to call my sister?" Uncle Jeff leaned back.

"Peachy," I said. "I'll be leaving tomorrow, but when I return, I'll explain everything."

The night was restless as I pondered a marriage of convenience. As I tossed and turned I thought, *Am I being wise? I could take the 235k I cleared and run. Head back to the south, pay cash for a house, and start over.*

A text from Rich lit my dark room.

RICH: *I'm out back. Let's take a walk.*

I threw on my sweats, bundled up in a blanket, and met him at the foot of the boardwalk. The specks of silver in his hair glistened from the night sky. More than his eyes. More than his moistened lips. "Shall we?" He reached his arm around me. "I haven't heard from you. I thought I would by now," he said. I looked straight ahead and avoided looking into his eyes. "What gives?"

"I should have held firm with my goodbye." I answered.

"I told you I love you and you disappeared." His voice cracked at the end.

"That night—a lot happened. You said you loved me, then I saw you checking out that blonde girl with the other men at the party. I mean I get it, men are going to look at women. But right after you profess your love?" My voice heightened. "I felt like you didn't mean it. Then I learned you have some sort of twisted history with the man who invited me. It felt like that whole dance was for show. Like you were using me to get under his skin."

"So that's what this is about. Charles Motherfucking Coppin." He stopped in his tracks.

"Care to explain?" I finally looked at him.

His long pause and slumped shoulders prepared me for his mistake. Finally, he was about to share something real about himself with me. "I had an affair with his wife and he refuses to let it go. My wife left me, his wife left him. It turned into this huge scandal around here years ago. Now we're supposedly sworn enemies."

I scoffed. "I met the wife at the gala."

His eyes stretched and he proceeded with our walk. "Your past has nothing to do with what happened between us. I just wanted you to know, that little bit of drama was put into my ear," I explained.

"Then why have you been avoiding me?" He glanced at me from the side of his eye.

"After my run in with that woman, I realized you and I wouldn't work. I set everything in play. I made the first move.

I was upfront with you about what happened between your son and I, and you played the background. You didn't fight for me. But I found someone who will."

"The wild card you've been hanging around with?"

I smiled. "Yeah. Him. I am deeply attracted to you, and might love you just a little bit." I teased him with my fingers. "I'm in love with him. In my own perfect world, I'd have you both."

"You mean like at the marina?" His voice croaked.

"Yeah, but all the time. The two men I love and desire taking care of my every need. Protecting me. Loving me."

"Are you desiring me right now?" He raised one eyebrow.

"I am. But I won't act on it. You still haven't taken me out once, and I have a big day tomorrow."

"Doing what?"

"Hopefully not making a mistake."

Rich's face scowled. He placed his hand in front of me and stopped my next step. "Now do you care to explain?"

"I can't go into detail, but after tonight, I can't see you anymore."

"Why the fuck not?"

I stood on my tiptoes and kissed him softly. The familiar taste of scotch and sweetness, and the manly wooden scent of cologne tipped my nipples under the blanket. "I...I better head back." I turned around and trekked back to the house with Rich on my heels calling out my name.

He hugged me from behind and begged to know why. The wind from the water and dancing sand wrapped around us. He spun me around to face him and held me by the face. "Tell me why." He demanded. I remained silent, met with his most passionate kiss, crushed between his arms.

"For what it's worth. I did love you," I said. "Goodbye."

I escaped back into the warmth and stared at the ceiling until the sun shone on my face. The day began with me behaving unlike myself. Before I rolled out of bed, I made a call I had been avoiding all summer. "Hello Mother."

"Well, I guess the south can expect snow this winter." She grumbled and breathed into the phone.

"I didn't call to argue. Just wanted to hear your voice," I said.

"Then something must be wrong."

"Nothing's wrong!" I exhaled and recomposed myself. "Sorry. I hate when you do this."

"Do what?"

Make me regret I called.

"Mom, I called to see how you are doing? Do you need anything?"

"Your uncle must have really blessed you."

"Something like that." I smirked to myself.

"Did that teacher ever get in touch with you?"

"He did." I pursed my lips.

"What are the men like out there? I would know for myself if your uncle ever invited me. He must find me repulsive."

"Actually, he told me you are his favorite sister. It's why he helped me."

She choked on her rebuttal. "Ha. I owe him an apology. I talked shit about him with the other two. So, how is he?"

"He's good. How are you?"

"You know me. Making what I have work." She sighed.

"I have an opportunity in Miami. I'll be in touch in a few days when I return."

"A job?" Mom inquired.

"Um, fingers crossed everything goes well. I have a few things lined up I need to run by you when I get back. Okay?"

"Listen to you. You sound so grown up. You be safe down there. Watch your drink." She disciplined in a stern tone.

"I will." I laughed. "I've *gotta* run now. Love you."

A reminder on my phone chimed. I dragged myself out of bed and dressed in a cream, fitted pants power suit. I pulled my hair in a low ponytail, and drew on a nude lip, then prepared for my flight while waiting for a confirmation from Phil about a list of errands I requested he handle once I was in the air.

Promptly at two o'clock a car arrived in front of Uncle Jeff's house. "I'll see you in a few days." I said.

My insides rumbled on the private jet parked on the tarmac. Coppin set his things a few rows ahead of me on the empty plane and talked business on the phone before liftoff. As the attendant prepared us for takeoff, I popped a Xanax I stole from the drawer of my mother's nightstand.

Temporarily suspending his calls, Coppin joined me on my row and checked my seatbelt. "Making sure the merchandise is protected." He joked.

All this man knows is property.

The jet rolled up the airstrip and Coppin placed his hand on my thigh. This time I didn't flinch. *Thank you, Xanax.* "Tell me, is my bride to be a member of the mile-high club?" I shook my head side to side. "You will be. We'll have flights like this to ourselves all the time."

"Mr. Coppin, I..."

He interjected. "Call me Charles." He grinned.

"Charles." I swallowed hard. "I neglected to negotiate my use of the plane," I said.

"What's one more amendment." He slapped my leg. "I was thinking of having you upgrade the manor down in the keys before you work on the house in the city."

"The Keys you say?"

"You'll have the house on the waterfront to yourself during the construction of course."

"And where will you be?" One of my eyebrows raised.

"In and out. Here and there. I won't be in your way. I'm a

busy man. There is a reason why the contract stated a quarterly hook-up. And why a man such as myself agreed to an open marriage as you young folk call it. Most people in my world understand affairs. It didn't need a label. Certain lines aren't to be crossed to make such arrangements work."

"Such as?"

"Falling in love with an outsider. Respecting public personas with the use of discretion. Understood?"

I turned to look at the clouds being cut by the wing of the jet, nodding my head and biting on my lower lip. "You aren't getting sweet on me already, are you?" He asked, gliding his finger up and down my leg.

I didn't dignify his silly question with a response. I kept staring out of the window thinking of my payday and the quickest way to consummate the sham. "How long is this engagement going to be?" I asked.

"Honey, I have friends in high places. A judge is waiting on us at the house. I'll be between those pretty brown legs and sucking on that sweet rose in a few hours." He moaned.

CHAPTER 25

Red Part Une

The plane landed in Miami. My first time in Florida. My first time as a bride. Whisked away by a chauffeured car to a house in Coral Gables amongst some of the city's elite figures. A house manager greeted us at the door of a mansion, as the staff removed our luggage from the car. "Judge Arthur is waiting for you in the library," he said.

Mr. Coppin...Charles, wasted no time to give me his last name. Before I was given a tour, a visit to the ladies' lounge, or **say** about when, where, and how we should exchange vows, he led me down an art filled hall with tall statues, high ceilings, and maple colored hardwood floors, into a study with books color coded from wall to wall. "Arthur, good to see you. I appreciate you coming over on such short notice." Said Charles, reaching for the judge's hand.

"Anything for you. And a wedding no less." He shook his hand. "You must be Amber." His eyes judged my age, but his smile approved.

Men.

"Nice to meet you," I said.

"Shall we get started?" Charles gestured with a warm nudge against my back.

In front of a shiny chestnut desk, Judge Arthur performed the ceremony of our nuptials. The glimmer in Charles's eyes made the blood in my veins dance and a shiver down my spine. His gaze never broke as I stood before him with a fake smile and stone heart. A diamond band was placed on my finger and the words, "I do," easily flowed from my mouth.

"I now pronounce you man and wife. You may kiss your bride."

Charles took me by surprise and dipped me. "Welcome to the good life," he said. His lips puckered and rested on mine for a short, sweet kiss. "Allow me to show you around your new home. At least one of them anyway." He grinned.

"After we sign, of course."

Judge Arthur signed the certificate and congratulated us on his way out. Charles escorted me through the house, out to the garden, around the pool and tennis court, then back inside towards the wing of the house where we would officially become husband and wife. "Are you nervous?" He asked, placing his jacket on the arm of the chair at the foot of the bed.

"No." I lied.

"Make yourself comfortable." He patted the spot next to him on the bed.

"Exactly how have you imagined this moment?" I remained standing.

"I'd rather show you than tell you," he said.

"Then show me."

I exhaled as he rose from the bed and grabbed onto my hands. A second delicate kiss landed on my lips, followed with the insertion of his tongue. He was nervous. And knowing this caused my jitters to settle, but my hands grew clammy in his. He knew all I saw was dollar signs when I looked at him, and was unbothered I didn't intertwine my tongue with his. He carried on with his desire and kissed me until I gave in and joined him in a lip lock. "It starts like that," he said.

"Then what?"

He undressed me slowly while I became familiar with the room. It was dark and old timey with paisley décor and expensive, ugly rugs. Once I was completely naked he stood back and stared at me in amazement. "You are every bit how I imagined." He said, pulled out a condom, and threw it on the bed.

Thank God.

He removed his clothing, then climbed next to the prophylactic. I blushed from his compliment and my nipples hardened from the draft circling the room. "Ooh," he moaned. "Come to me Mrs. Coppin."

I crossed both feet, climbed next to him and closed my eyes. He fondled my breasts with his lips and his fingers, then licked them with his tongue. The sound of my gasps excited him. His old cock sprung forward against my thigh and I stiffened. My curious eyes opened to see what he looked like.

Damn. Not bad for a man his age.

"Touch it," he said.

I placed my hand around his cock and jerked him mid-tempo. He sighed and *ah'd* for a few seconds, then stopped my hands in motion. "In my vision, you touch yourself. Go ahead. Get that pussy wet for me."

I giggled. "This pussy is always wet."

"Oh baby. I didn't know you had a mouth like that on you." He grinned.

I spread my legs, then my brown folds, and tapped my exposed tan clit with two fingers to tease him. His dick twitched in his hands. Those two fingers rubbed my hood until the pink of my clit blossomed. I circled it until my fingers glistened with my slick, then tapped on it with soft slaps. "Is this how you imagined it?"

"Even better." His tongue hung from his mouth.

He dove forward and placed his tongue inside my cavern, curving it upward and licked until he rang the bell. *Oh shit he went straight for the g-spot.* I shook and wriggled, held wide by his thumbs. His mouth covered my entrance and he plastered his face against my nook, shaking uncontrollably until I shrieked. Up and down his tongue stroked. "Mmm. It's so beautiful. Tastes good too." He hummed.

Images of my past weeks in Malibu flashed in my head. Chase, Rich, and Professor Kelte, all in on the fun this lucky bastard was now about to experience.

Charles snacked on my goods as if he had practiced a routine of what he would do to me when given the chance. "Don't stop," I begged. He hummed and sang as he rolled the latex down his pipe. I gyrated in his mouth and he mumbled indistinctly munching below my shaved carpet.

He lunged inside and I held my breath. I was prepared to fake enjoyment, but when he plunged inside, my walls relaxed and received him. He started with a slow grind. His face buried itself against my shoulder while he held my legs up with his forearms. "Sweet heavens," he whispered.

He dug and drilled until I shrieked and my pussy clamped around his cock. I unloaded on him but he was still in play. *It's gotta be the barrier of the condom, or he popped a pill when I wasn't looking.*

He lifted his head and smiled at my breasts bouncing near his lips. He nibbled on them and I panted from his remaining stamina for the next five minutes. As I was for the taking, he hunched and grunted growing weaker by the second. "Two years." He huffed. "Renegotiate." He said and came with a gurgling sound expelling from his lips.

Easiest 500k I'm ever going to make. Again, THANK YOU Xanax.

He rolled over and peeled the condom from his cock and threw it on the floor. "Best decision of my life," he said.

Damn. All I did was masturbate and moan. What would he have thought if I was really into it?

He slid down my body with kisses until he reached my toes, then kissed my feet. He sat up and drew pressurized circles on them. "You can hire someone to do this for you. I don't know why I felt the need to, but here I am kissing and rubbing your feet." He giggled.

I lied on my back with my eyes closed, grinning from his manual labor until he hurdled over the bed and grabbed his phone from his jacket. With the push of a button the phone dialed his accountant. "Do it." He said, then lied down next to me. "I kept my word. I hope you keep yours," he said. "I'll have your bags brought in. Get dressed. We're going on a helicopter ride over the city and down to the keys. I want to show you the property you'll be renovating before I leave in the morning."

"Leave?"

"I knew you were getting attached to me." He chuckled. "I told you I'm gone quite often."

He dressed and left me lying on the bed. Before the staff brought in my luggage, I checked for the pending balance in my account, then texted Phil for an update.

PHIL: *Papers delivered. How are you?*

Married. :ME

PHIL: *You are officially richer than me. How does it feel?*

Uncertain. How did he take it? :ME

PHIL: *He ran after my car. Are you really okay?*

_ :ME

Charles was a man of his word. I was paid every time thus far without a hassle, well taken care of, and now living a life of lonely luxury. A quarterly romp in the hay felt well worth the sacrifice.

The property in the Keys was sure to keep me busy, and it appeared to be by design. As the week ended of countless meetings with contractors, visits to home stores, and working with Coppin's property managers about scheduling, I wasn't needed in Florida for a few months.

Phil and I met at the airport in Shreveport. "Ah! A familiar face!" I said, reaching to hug him. "Thank you for coming."

"What's a rich gal like you doing flying commercial?" He raised his brow.

"It still hasn't quite registered yet." I blushed. "Ready to go make an old gal happy?" I joked.

"It's why I'm here."

An impromptu surprise visit to my old house on the south side grounded me. Memories of competing in everything from academics to athletics to be the *"one"* to make it out of there brought a smile to my face.

As Phil pointed out, I no longer lived this life, but its struggles and teachings would forever be engraved in my bones. I studied Phil's face the closer the car arrived at my childhood home. "Hard to believe the girl you thought was the next big thing came from a place like this, huh?" I asked him.

"Diamonds come from the ground don't they," he said.

My mother's mouth dropped at the sight of me, then her

face crumpled at the sight of Phil. "Who is this?" I hugged her and invited Phil inside. "I would have tidied up if I knew you were coming home. You look good girl." She laughed, then shifted her eyes back to Phil. "Now who is this?"

"Mom, this is my friend and lawyer Phil."

Phil nodded and shook her hand. "Amber is as pretty as her mother I see." His mouth salivated.

"Stop that. I will not have you as my step-father," I said.

"Why not?" My mother asked.

"He knows why." I muttered.

I eyed them both as I stepped towards the kitchen and the three of us laughed. Searching for leftovers in the fridge I shouted, "Why is the refrigerator so empty?" I peaked at my mother over the door and saw her throat take a huge swallow. She folded her hands together and her eyes looked away. I knew that look. She didn't have any money. I said under my breath, "This is exactly why I took Charles's deal."

Phil didn't need to be from my neck of the woods to figure out what was going on. The look of pity was all over his face. Mom looked at me ashamed. "I'm on my way back to California. I hope my surprising you with company hasn't upset you," I said.

"No. It's always good to have you home. Even though this place was never good enough for you. Lord knows you couldn't wait to get up *outta* here." She looked at Phil and said, "She practically ran off to college. And stayed gone for the summer." She tapped the back of Phil's hand.

She can never know the man calling the house was the reason I was gone every summer.

"Put on something nice. We're taking you out before our flight leaves."

"I don't go to the casino anymore. The wrong men hang out there."

"Where I'm taking you, the last thing you'll need to worry about is a man, Mom."

She reached and felt my forehead. "Not worry about a man? You don't feel like you have a fever," she said. We stared into each other's eyes and chuckled. Phil stood by oblivious to what was being said between us. Only women who had been in our shoes would have picked up on the joke.

Mom looked at me in amazement inside the car, taken aback by the chauffeur and luxury of the vehicle. We entered a quiet little neighborhood north of the city, closer to her job, and away from the base. "Welcome home," I said. Phil handed her the keys to her new home. "It's all yours. I'll take care of everything from here on out. Whatever you choose to do with your money is up to you," I said.

"If this house is mine, the last thing a man is going to do is take his shoes off in it," she said.

"Enjoy." Phil added, handing her an envelope with a copy of the deed with her name on it, and banking information.

The tears in her eyes made mine water. *Damn, I wasn't prepared to cry.* She and I went inside with Phil on our heels. "Fix it up however you like. There is a card inside the envelope Phil gave you. Use it as you wish." I kissed her on the cheek.

"My darling daughter, I love you. I love this house. But what did you do?" Her eyes narrowed at me.

"I got married," I said. "To a very wealthy man."

She took me by the hand and stared at my ring finger. "I thought this ring was a fashion statement." She turned to Phil. "Are you my new son-in-law?"

"No ma'am. Someone else beat me to the punch." Phil scoffed.

"Then when do I meet him?" Mom looked confused.

"I'll fly you out soon. Once the house is renovated. You'll have your own room and everything. Enjoy the beach. Get some sun. Go shopping and get massages. Things are going to be different from here on out." I squeezed her hand.

"One last question." Mom asked, "When can I rub this in my sister's faces?!"

My return back to Malibu was kept under the radar. As the contractors worked on the house, I stayed with Uncle Jeff making the neighbors question if the rumor was true Charles and I were wed, or if I was simply upgrading his home.

Uncle Jeff's demeanor changed towards me once he heard the news. I narrowed down his emotions to either shame because of the age difference, disappointment because I didn't discuss my plan with him, outrage his friend pounced on his favorite niece, and hurt because I chose wealth over love.

"Are you happy?" he asked.

"I am."

"How? You were into that crazy boy with the nice cars and bad attitude." He shook his head.

"I'm sorry to worry you. Charles offered what he couldn't. You remember what it's like to want and dream, don't you? Or has this plentiful lifestyle caused you to forget?"

My uncle piped down and turned pensive. I assumed reflecting on his life before he struck it rich and forgot about us back in the south. He exhaled deeply and placed his hand on his hip. "I suppose I have forgotten what it's like. It is nice to have the things you want in life versus wishing for them. Unfortunately, everything comes with a price and a sacrifice. And I hate you felt the need to sacrifice true love for material things."

"Food and shelter aren't material. They are necessities withheld by the almighty dollar. Which I have now."

"Very true, but you sacrificed three loves. And the way they all behaved after finding out what you did, I believe you had a chance of having a good life. One with love and happiness. Sometimes those two things outweigh wealth." He pursed his lips.

"Why do you say that?"

"The crazy one came by here and had a long conversation with me about how much he loves you. He wanted to cry. I'm sure of it. My golf buddy looked like he had seen a ghost, and the stalker one didn't stop coming around until I told him you ran off and got married. And he looked like someone ripped his heart out. I believe he wanted to cry too."

Uncle Jeff looked out the window and shook his head. "Come see for yourself. The poor bastard is sitting outside right now."

CHAPTER 26

Red Part Deux

K elte hopped out of his car when he saw me spring down the stairs on the porch. He leaned against the driver side door, charming me with his boyish good looks and mouth twisted to the side.

I leaned against the car on the passenger side and grinned at him across the roof. "What's up?" I raised my brows.

"Who's the lucky guy?" He glared at me.

"You don't know him."

"So, it's true?" His eyes widened and he tapped the roof of the car with his keys.

"Yeah. It's true." I pressed my lips together.

"After I told you I loved you."

"You don't love me. You miss the idea of me being in love with you. I do want us to be friends." I posed with praying hands.

"You and I can never be friends. We'll always be more than that. Call me when you're done playing house."

The next day I attended a luncheon as a favor for one of Charles's many charities. *Women Wear Red* received a hefty check from him every year. As the woman of the house, it was the first of my appearances on his list.

I ditched the power suit look and represented him the way he wished in a red tailored sheath dress and red bottoms, turning heads for more reasons than one.

I returned to the house to oversee the work of the contractors and check in with his secretary, Shia, suffering from the noise. "I don't know why you insist on being here in the midst of all this racquet. You can work from home for the rest of the week." I offered.

"It's louder at my house," she said. "A package arrived for you this morning by courier. I placed it on the desk in Mr. Coppin's office."

"Thank you. Take a long lunch. I'll hang out here until you get back." I shooed her out of the house.

The rectangular package sitting on the desk was wrapped in brown paper, on top of turquoise Tiffany's paper. "What has Charles sent me?" I whispered and smiled to myself. I opened the case and the smile disappeared from my lips as my eyes rested on a full string of pearls.

I panicked and hesitated to read the card. The agreement ran across my mind. Millions were at stake. My newfound way of life threatened.

I went to the window of the office and looked in the direction of Rich's house. No sign of him. I unfolded the card and read his words:

Dearest Amber,
You were right. I didn't fight for you, but I want to now, if it's not too late. If the rumors are true, and I hope they aren't, I will accept my loss and wait for you as you once waited for me. Please accept this gift as a token of my love for you. What kind of man would I be if I didn't honor you with a real set of Akoya Pearls. Your very own strand and something to remember me by. But nothing will ever be as memorable as the first set. ~ Yours truly

I lifted the velvet box and unhooked the pearls, placing them between my teeth as I stared at his house, then fastened them around my neck. Tracing each bead with my fingers, I ran scenarios in my head of how I could thank him. How I wanted to thank him. Each frame played out disastrously in the end.

With the pearls still around my neck, I clutched them and closed the drapes, then hid the wrapping paper in my tote. My chest pounded as I re-read the note a second time.

Rich, you will not fuck up my money. Why would you send these here? Charles was right. You can't be trusted. Sneaky asshole.

I shredded the card at Shia's desk, pulled the pieces from the pile, and threw them in my purse; In desperate need of a breather, I returned to Charles's office and closed the door. As I stepped towards the desk, the door creaked behind me. "Shia, you can take the rest of the day off. I'd like to be left alone please." I said, leaning against the polished wood.

"I've never seen you in red." His voice whispered with sincerity.

I lifted my head and turned around. "Chase," I exclaimed in a whisper as my shoulders sunk and my heart sang.

"I missed you baby," he said.

"What are you doing here?" I asked, smiling at him.

"Pretending to be one of the crew." He locked the door. "I

see you missed me too." He dashed towards my nipples greeting him through my dress.

He pinned me against the desk. My pussy throbbed and I winced. "Chase, we can't."

"Oh yes we can. Your errand boy dropped off the papers. I'm a part of this charade. He's a fool to let you have an open marriage. I would never share you with anyone. I should kill him so you can be all mine again." He said lifting my dress to my hips.

Chase plastered his full lips on mine, hard and rough. Our mouths grazed one another, tasting the lustful desire between us once more. I panted into his mouth and squirmed in his arms, yearning for him to put the fire out between my thighs. "Not here," I said.

"Why not? This old bastard stole something from me. It's only right I have **my** way with you in **his** house." He rubbed my vulva with the bone in his wrist.

"You're making it hard for me to say no." I sighed.

"Then say yes. That old fucker *ain't* handling his business. I can tell." He smirked.

Yes. I need it. I haven't been touched in weeks.

"Fucking you will cost me a million dollars," I muttered.

His wrist stopped rotating and he backed away. "You're worth more than a million dollars to me Chica. Why don't you know that? You really are in the dark. You have no idea who my father was. I'm not broke. I could have given you a great life." He paced the floor.

"I'm sorry for what I've done." I exhaled and lowered my dress. "I want to be with you. Just not here. Meet me at that hotel in Santa Barbara tonight. I'll text you the room number."

"Do I need to bring anything?" Chase asked, holding my chin between his fingers.

A curve formed on the side of my mouth. "Gifts are always welcome."

He kissed my lips gently and smiled, then disappeared into the hallway. I huffed and caught my breath, fanning myself to cool down. I took a moment for myself and parked in Coppin's chair, shaking my head at the life I created, then laughed out loud as I asked Shia to check into the hotel and bring the three keys back to the office.

Good dick is hard to give up. Pun intended.

Shia returned to the house with the room keys and asked no questions. *Coppin taught her well.* "There's a bonus in the top drawer of your desk. Thank you for running this errand at the last minute for me. See you tomorrow."

She nodded.

I retreated to Uncle Jeff's house and threw the courier box and wrapping paper in the garbage, then lit a quick fire on the pit out on the upper deck. Piece by piece, I tossed the shredded note into the fire. "Goodbye Rich." I said under my breath.

With an overnight bag thrown over my shoulder, I drove Uncle Jeff's spare car to my rendezvous, and set myself up in the room on the seventh floor. Candles were lit, wine was uncorked, and weeks of abandonment awaited me.

I texted Chase: *Room 202.*

Two hours later I messaged The Professor my location: *You want it. Come and get it. Don't show up empty handed.*

Chase took his time coming to me. He knocked on the door and I jumped off the bed completely bare to let him in. He eyed me up and down with a large box wrapped in gold paper and a shiny golden ribbon in his hands.

He hesitated coming inside. My nipples rippled at the

scent of his cologne teasing me to taste him. My thighs twitched from my yoni practicing jumping jacks at the sight of him. "Is making me wait your way of punishing me," I said.

"Who the fuck do you think you are, questioning me of my whereabouts after denying me **MY** pussy." His face bared no emotion.

"Then go back home." I motioned to close the door.

He placed his hand on the door, pushed it towards me and came inside. I stepped backwards with my eyes fixated on the anger in his. He placed the box on the table. "Come here," he commanded. I stood still. "I said come here." He voiced in a softer tone, calling me over with his finger. I stood before him. He lifted my face and kissed me delicately. "What do you want?"

"You," I said.

"No. You want my cock in your mouth. On your knees."

He placed his hand on my shoulder and lowered me to the floor. I sacrificed my knees on the carpet and released his protruding bulge and opened my mouth. He shoved his dick in my mouth and held it at the back of my throat in a stronghold. I held my breath and slid my tongue side to side on his sack, tapping on his hips to pull back. I panted for air and looked up at him. *You in danger girl*, I said to myself fearing the rage of his furrowed brows.

"Who told you to stop?" He said, shoving his cock back inside my mouth. *Ooh, he's angry.* "Ah," he exhaled, fucking my throat with a vengeance until a tear dropped from one of my eyes.

He wiped it away and lifted me from the floor. "Mi dulzura." He whispered and followed with a tender kiss then gazed into my eyes. "When you asked me how I felt about marriage, I should have driven us to Vegas and made you mine. Why did you do this to us Chica?"

I turned my head and shrugged. He lifted me and threw

me on the bed. Still angry. Still vengeful. "Put your legs together." He ordered and I obeyed. "Look at that beautiful pussy. Begging to be watered." He licked it slow and soft on the sides. I wiggled from the warmth of his tongue. He bear hugged my thighs to keep me in place and lathered my orifice with licks, nibbles, and tongue strokes circling in my pink.

I hollered for him to fuck me, called out to God, and cupped my breast in euphoric agony of his punishment. "That's right. You're *gonna* beg for this dick. Suck it again." He pulled me up and shoved his wood back into my mouth. I moaned with him placed on my tongue and swished him from cheek to cheek. His leg muscles stiffed against my palms, so I swished his dick side to side again then sucked him with the roof of my mouth like a lollipop. "Yes. Like that," he growled. "Just like that."

I rolled his tip near my throat canal, then slid him all the way in my mouth from his head to the bottom of his base. He grunted and jerked, so I used the technique of sound to weaken him, and popped my lips when I set him free. He shook in my hands, lifted me to my feet, and bent me over the edge of the bed, stuffing his nose so far up my ass I considered it breached. His tongue took deep long strides, covering every inch of my hidden lips it could reach. Beneath him I squeezed a pillow and muffled my moans, ready to be penetrated. "Yes," I belted, and vibrated from his entry, gasping of the pain and pleasure I desperately missed.

His curved cocked offered no mercy on me. He rolled his hips, poked, and prodded into the spots only he had reached within my walls. "Rain on me dulzura." He moaned. "Rain on me dulzura." My ass cheeks jiggled and my pussy throbbed on his imperious cock. *Smack!* His palms spanked each cheek. *Smack!* I felt his anger in his strike.

As I came he pulled me up by my hair and ferociously stroked me from behind, wrapping the other hand around my neck. "I fucking loved you bitch. I still love you. You fucked me over punta." He whined, choking me. "You were mine. Eras mia." His voice cracked as he bit my ear mildly. "Turn around." He said pulling out.

I gasped for air as I faced him. His hand gently brushed my shoulder, then guided me to sit on the bed while the other stroked his cock until it was at my eye level. He cradled my head with both hands and fucked my mouth. With short breaths I survived his cock rage, salivating from the sides of my mouth, then trapping his wang with a closed mouth and holding his head between the tunnel of my throat. He exploded inside. "I...I..." he cried, pulsating against my tongue.

Fuck with his head. Do what the professor showed you.

I opened my mouth and released him, gazed deep into his eyes, and blew a bubble slowly. Chase's eyes grew big and his mouth dropped open. I took the tip of his penis and burst it, rendering him senseless. "Show off." He held the smile hiding behind his emotions and stood above me, gazing back into my eyes. Loving me, but hating me all the same.

I excused myself to the bathroom and freshened up. When I returned to the bedroom, Chase stood fully dressed with his hands in his pocket. "I bought that for you the day you left." He tilted his head towards the box, then took my hand and placed a key in the center of my palm. "Here's my real gift. Next time you come to me."

I carried the box to my room, wowed at its contents. A diamond tennis bracelet to match the studs he bought me was hooked on the strap of a taupe Etoupe Birkin bag.

The fuck have I done.

I gulped a glass of red wine, then showered and fell

asleep in The Professor's room with Chase on my mind. Accepting I sacrificed a decent, happy life with him for a plush life with Charles. But I didn't cry. The only tear I dropped was the one of pleasure he wiped away.

Professor Kelte finally arrived at 3 a.m. He climbed into bed and snuggled against me. I was still wet and swollen from the beating in Room 202, but he delivered extra saturation to my slit. I huffed and exhaled, jerking from arousal while holding his head in place. Familiar with my routine, The Professor fast stroked my clit with his tongue and massaged the sides of my pussy with his saturated thumbs. When I came he applied pressured to the points he massaged and I stiffened in place as my pussy contracted and released. "*Thata* girl." He said, inhaling my aroma and rubbing his nose against my folds.

His mouth traced my skin from my navel to my breast. "Don't tap out on me now Berry." He grazed each of my nipples with his teeth. The hair on my arms raised and my shoulders rolled from the sensation. He slipped inside and groaned. "The thought of not having this pussy tortures me at night." He said, squeezing my ass and sucking on my neck. I welcomed his thrust, and spent the next fifteen minutes *slow-whined* beneath him with my feet touching the headboard. "You miss that?" He asked.

"Yes," I purred.

"What else do you miss?" He dug deeper.

"The toys." I admitted.

He placed his hand in my mouth for a few seconds and removed it. "Which ones?" He pounded harder.

"The flogger." I whined.

"What else?" He grazed my neck with his teeth.

"The whip." I sighed.

"Next time." He slapped my breast.

I moaned of intrigue.

"I promise." He slapped the edge of my nipple harder.

He slid me to the edge of the bed and fed his cock to my mouth as my head hung upside down. "You miss this?" He asked. I moaned and nodded my head. "Taste your sweet pussy," he said. Nice and slow he downward fucked my mouth, grunting when I squeezed my jaws every time he pulled it out. "Yes. Yes. Yes. You remember how I like it. Suck that dick baby." He deepthroated me, wiggling his head around my tonsils.

I slid my head down towards the carpet and rolled my feet to the floor. The Professor scoffed and dove his mouth to my asshole. He plugged my hole with his tongue and serviced it sensuously. "Who else has been there?" He asked when he rose for air. "Tell me to take it." He begged, circling my slit with his thumb.

"Not tonight." I said, studying his smooth, thick penis jolting every few seconds.

He spread his legs and positioned inside my aching apex. Stroking me wide and scraping my vessel like a cavity. As he toured my lines and grooves, I moistened my fingers and massaged his perineum, then his balls pressed against my clit. "Stop," he groaned. "You're going to make me blast."

He pulled out and licked my center, tasting the nectar he juiced. "Let me see those pretty tits bounce." He maneuvered my body on top of his. I exhaled a sigh of joy at his penetration, and rode him like the bull he was. He laid back with his hands behind his head, and beamed at my breasts springing up and down, encouraging me to keep the perfect pace I was treading. "Take that dick." He grinned.

Unable to keep his hands off of me, he pinched my nipples, then rolled his palms around them. "I missed that," I said. One by one his fingers traced my areolas, then moved down to my folds where he briefly played with my clit.

After watching me throw my hair back and get off on his

skillful hands, Kelte placed them on my ass and handed me the assist, guiding my pussy round and round on his pipe.

I liked that move.

"I'm coming," I crooned.

"I feel it trickling Princess," he said, rubbing my clitoris with his fingers until I came. "Keep fucking that dick. Don't let that nut stop you," he ordered.

I slowed down to catch a breath and he wasn't having it. He flipped me over and held my hips, hardcore stroking me on my knees with my ass in the air. Retaining a handful of my strands in his fist, Kelte leaned down and breathed out against my back, then ran his hands against my scalp until my hair tie fell out. "Unh," I panted from the pressure.

He unfolded my knees and lifted me into a wheelbarrow. I clung to the sheets, retracting to every thrust he jabbed. My body fell to the mattress. The Professor pressed his hand in the small of my back, deep stroking me every time I attempted to lift my head. His palm traveled north and pressed my head against the sheets, as the other gripped my shoulder, forcefully nurturing his aching lumber into my tunnel.

His cock pulsated side to side and stirred when he expelled. His head stretched wider inside of me as he released. I rolled my ass elongating the moment of nostalgia between us before he removed himself. He gently bit the center of my back, then kissed my spine until he reached my backdoor, and swirled his tongue around my exit.

When he finished licking me clean, he kissed each of my cheeks and sounded off. "Muah." I rolled to the middle of the bed and covered my body with the sheets.

Kelte lifted his pants from the floor and pulled out his wallet. "If you put cash on the nightstand I'll slap you," I said. He laughed and held up a joint.

"I didn't know what to get you this late."

He placed the pre-rolled spliff between his lips and lit the tip, then inhaled. Parting his mouth halfway to curve the smoke towards his nose. "I see you're draped in diamonds and pearls and shit. How can I keep up?" His eyes studied my jewels with a grin of approval on his lips as he puffed a second toke and exhaled.

"You better figure that out if you want this to happen again."

I patted the bed for him to join me. He grinned on the side of his mouth and hovered over me. "Open up," he said, blowing smoke into my mouth. I held it and released, then took the spliff from his hands.

"Take this necklace off of me." I asked before inhaling my first toke. "Trade it, pawn it, hawk it. I don't care. But bring me something better next time we meet."

Kelte unfastened the necklace and grazed the beads with his teeth. "I have an idea of how to use them first." He said, kissing my naked body and rolling the strand against my skin as I smoked. "We were meant for each other. You and me." He groaned, tonguing my torso and tracing the outline of my swollen chasm with the pearls.

While nibbling on my hood and rubbing my dark tunnel with the necklace, The Professor asked, "Whose pussy is this?" I blew a cloud of smoke above me in the air and answered.

"Mine."

About the Author

For updates, sequel information, reading order of my work, and upcoming giveaways, subscribe to my newsletter:
https://diannejune.ck.page

For more information about Dianne June
and to shop for merchandise visit:

https://diannejune.square.site

Join my reader group:

www.facebook.com/groups/diannesdiehards

Amber & Chase

A Follow-up Novella

And

A Very Merry X-Mess

Coming Soon

The Professor & I

The Pecking Order

A sneak peek into the follow-up novella,

Amber & Chase

(Image Shown Is An Optional Alternate Cover For Print.)

Amber & Chase

CHASE

She better show up. I'd hate to punish one of these unsuspecting housewives out here on vacation and fuck up her life. *'They always get attached.'* The one housewife I'd make the exception for, ran off and got attached to old money. And I still want her.

It's been a year since Amber took the old man's name and benched me to the sideline. We've fucked twice since I gave her the key to my house. Even though she left me high and dry with my heart hanging on a string, I can't get over her. No woman has ever made me a fool for love, until now.

She replied to my text saying she would get away for the weekend and spend lovers' day with me. Valentine's Day has never meant anything to me before, but another day for the one percent to capitalize on hard earned money from the lower class. But this year it would mean everything to me, if Amber chooses to spend it with me and tell me she still loves me.

I've been here for a few hours and jump from the bed every time I hear a car door close. This suite is decked out with all the bells and whistles, but will be a waste if I have to enjoy it alone. I have Chandon on ice, white roses by the bedside, and chocolate flown in from Belgium. She posted how much she loved it from this place out there when she was on vacation with her husband. *'Prick.'*

It's hard to know what I can give her since she has everything a woman could want: servants, money, houses, and cars.

Blades from a chopper outside my window whirr, and I dash to the window. The snow dances in the wind as the force of the helicopter clears a spot to land. The owner, Clark, stands in the entrance with a woman, both covered in Sherpa lined coats holding hands.

The whirring of the chopper slowly comes to a halt and the rear door opens. Four inch heeled boots with red paint on the bottom imprint the snow, and my heart stops. Amber. Arriving like the first lady she is in style captivates my world, and I smile like an idiot losing all of my cool.

I'm nervous and I'm tripping. *'Get it together,'* I tell myself, watching her big smile thank the pilot from above. *'I should go down and greet her at the front desk. No. Chill and stop being lame. She likes the tough guy. So be the tough guy.'*

The pilot escorts her out of the snow until she stands below the drop off zone. My dick is harder than a brick watching her tight jeans show off her ass where the hem of her white fur stops perfectly in place. She shakes the hands of the lodge owners while the pilot returns to the helicopter, and retrieves her bags. Stacking them like Jenga pieces.

I pace back and forth, waiting to hear her heels clank against the shiny hardwood. I add another block of wood to keep the fire going as one minute— two minutes go by. Finally, I hear her strutting down the hall. I step back as she approaches the door with her key in hand. She hesitates and the back of my neck tightens. "Turn it love. Come on in," I whisper.

The lock twists horizontally and the door creaks open. I stand with the tips of my fingers tucked inside my pocket.

"Breathtaking," I say and curve the side of my mouth.

She stands with the door open behind her and surveys the room. I'm sure it is up to par with her luxurious lifestyle. With her lips slightly parted she removes her rose tinted shades and smiles at me. I eliminate any space between us and steal her mauve painted lips with a delicate kiss.

I reach behind her and shut the door. Her bags fall to the floor as I knock them out of our way and press her sexy ass against the coated wood. She moans in my mouth and I in hers. Her fur falls to her feet as I ravish her suffering body. It needs my touch.

Hot and heavy we exchange passionate kisses hunching up and down the door. She unbuckles my belt, making it slap when she throws it against the wall. I pause my urgency and look into her begging brown eyes and wet mouth smirking at me.

"Damn girl I missed you." I breathe into her mouth.

"Show me," she says.

I lift her sweater from her body with one hand and force the other between her unbuttoned jeans and silk panties. My hand palms her viscous pussy and she sighs, twitching it open and closed in my grip.

Gasping at the anticipation of her wet folds finally within my reach, I rest my head upon her shoulder while my fingers slide her thin protective layer to the side. "You grew it out for me I see." I grip on the full bush sprouting above her cave. She grins on the side of her mouth and melts like butter when my fingers touch her center. I swear I can already feel how fucking good her warmth is from the touch.

Her muscles contract around my fingers and I lose control. I thrust them fast, hard and deep inside her walls, panting against her neck. She moans of ecstasy and my mouth tastes the gardenia perfume from her neck. I suck and I pull to leave my mark.

"Now," she orders me.

I fall to my knees and lower her glued on jeans above hers, then taste the juice my tongue yearned for these past months. "Mmm," I moan aloud for her to hear the satisfaction she brings me. "This Grade A pussy is sweeter than cake," I mutter as I lick.

"What's that?" She respires.

Unable to stop pleasing her throbbing center, I neglect to repeat myself and circle my tongue around her clit. Her finger joins me at the top and pats her flesh for more friction. "I can't take it any longer," I say, then rise from the floor and turn her pretty face towards the wood.

"Ah," she squeals when I plunge inside like a bullet being shot from a gun.

Her sugar walls welcome me with graciousness. They squeeze my pipe, and pulse all around it upon my entry. The sensation is so intense, I freeze with my tip massaging the apex of her canal. Amber's hand slaps the door from the pleasurable pain.

"Hold it back," she whispers.

"I can't make any promises right now. You know you're holding some serious heat between those thighs."

She grins as best she could with her face pressed against the entrance to the room. Her soft cheeks lift for me to apply more pressure. I pull my dick out and lung back in harder, and hold it steady until I feel the rain of her pink pillowy clouds.

"Come on," she demands.

'It's go time.'

Squeezing her shoulders, I lean back and maneuver her ass back and forth. Her groans ascend louder, causing footsteps outside our room to linger.

"Don't stop," she begs.

"I couldn't if I was paid to," I utter.

The head on my third leg takes control, and I fuck her without remorse or care. Amber's hands rise above her head against the door, her nails scratching into the wood. The sound would normally drive me crazy, but the moment of lust and passion drowns out the annoyance.

I bite the back of her shoulder lightly, and fight myself to regain control. "Uh!" I shriek as I pull out my dick and bust into my palm.

"You alright back there big boy?" She jokes.

"No," I say, struggling to catch my breath.

Amber turns to face me and smiles. Her hair is less intact and her brown skin is glowing. I caress her face and kiss her, then brush my cheek against hers.

"That was quite an entrance you made," I say.

She chuckles. "Jealous?"

"A little bit." I laugh. "I'm so glad you came."

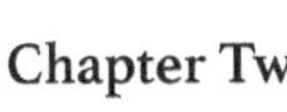

Chapter Two
Amber

'He better have greeted me with fire.'

"Four months and you finally reach out to me. Does this mean you're not mad at me anymore?" I say as I fully undress and fall back onto the bed.

He hovers above me then toys with my nipples. His breath tickles the center of my torso on his way down to my navel, reluctant to answer, and I know why. He will forever be mad at me for my haste, but can't resist the dynamic connection we share when we're together. My desire matches his freak.

I run my fingers through his low haircut. My nails graze his scalp and he grows weak, and lays his head on my stomach.

"Do you make those social media posts because you know I'm checking to see what you're up to? Or are you just living your best life, and not thinking of me at all?" He asks, staring up at me to influence my response.

I chuckle. "What do you think?"

"Are we going to play this game all weekend? Answer questions with questions?" I jump as his teeth graze my lower stomach.

Moaning and tracing my outer abdomen with gentle brushes, his teeth retreat and his lips kiss me softly where his teeth scuffed my skin.

"If I remember correctly, you are the master at other games. Games I like to play. None of this tit for tat shit that led to you not talking to me for months."

"What have you been doing since I saw you last? Besides traveling the world in style, and being the prettiest woman to walk the earth."

"You'd be proud. I've invested in a company or two, and I'm working on creating a brand to call my own."

"A brand? Doing— Making— Selling what?"

"Lingerie and swimwear."

Chase lifts his head and smiles at me showing all of his teeth. I stare down at him and raise my brows.

"What?"

"You're right. I am proud of you. But…"

"But what?"

"You could have done all of that with me."

I give him the old tap on the shoulder men should be smart enough to know is not a compliment, and roll from beneath him. I stand at the window and open the drapes, exposing my naked body to anyone lucky enough to see. A shuttle and a black car approach the chalet in the distance, and a group of men smoking down in the resort's courtyard below are too engaged with one another to pay me any mind.

Chase jumps from the bed and spreads his arms out wide, closing the curtains with a quick tug. He wrapped his arms around me and held me captive with his overpowering strength.

"What did I say that was so wrong? It's the truth and you know it. You just don't want to admit you made a mistake. All you have to do is leave him and we can pick up where we left off." He muffles in my ear.

"Are you done? Because I am. So glad I didn't waste my time unpacking. It was sort of good seeing you Chase," I say emotionless, squirming to free myself of him.

"If I have to chain you in this room and gag you I will. You're not running away from me this time."

"Sadly, I believe you would do some crazy shit like that."

"And you'd love every minute of it," he says, then spins me around to face him. "Tell me I'm wrong."

I place my fingers to his temple and nudge him out of my space. He laughs and falls backwards onto the bed. His chest is pounding so profusely I swear I hear it beat as if it's next to my face. He places his hands to cover his face, and mutters something low in his palms indistinctly.

"What was that?" I ask.

"I meant what I said the first time we hooked up."

"You say a lot of things."

"When I said if I had to choose my death it would be fucking you. I'd choose this every time. I miss you."

The bass in his voice trembles as he confesses his feelings. I already know he misses me. I miss him too. I even think of what my life would be like if I had chosen his unpredictable, jealous, crazy ass over Charles. I ask myself would I be happier, if there was such a thing. Would I have peace?

Would I regret submitting to his possessiveness? Would choosing him have been smarter because we love each other?

It is true, he loves me and is madly in love with me— And the way he fucks me is incomparable to any of my other lovers. But the extra zero attached to Coppin's last name wins me over every time I ask myself the hard questions.

'Money truly has turned me into such a heartless bitch.'

"I miss you too," I say to calm him.

"Come here. I want to feel you in my arms every minute I have you to myself."

I oblige and lay on top of him. "What do you have planned for us to do this weekend?"

"Tonight, you and I are scheduled to go on a romantic, late-night sleigh ride, but I'm thinking we should cancel everything and never leave this room."

"Um. Come again. Me in the cold ass snow at night on a sleigh? I'll pass."

"It's supposed to be fun. And popular. It's on a path that leads to a hidden restaurant with a world renowned chef. I thought you would love to try it with all of your latest travels. Has marriage stolen your sense of adventure?" His fingers trace the inner flesh of my ass.

"Can't we just have the helicopter drop us off to this place?" I squeeze my cheeks tight and laugh.

"You'd like that wouldn't you? And no. I'm not stepping inside of anything your husband owns."

"Too late." I kid.

"So he owns you now?" His voice struggles to hide the fact he's irritated from my joke.

"No one owns me, but he does have papers on me."

"Not for long Amber Edmonds. Soon to be Amber Alonso."

Chase closes his eyes and smiles to himself. I imagine he was thinking saying such a thing out loud would make it come true. As much as I would love to give him what he wants, it pains me to know I'm not changing my mind about my decision.

Over the past few months, I've grown accustomed to married life, and my duties as a billionaire's wife. A billionaire who cosigns our open marriage, and allows me the freedom to do whatever I want, when I want.

A marriage to Chase would have been quite the opposite. I would have access to his money, but limited. I would not have any freedom, constant tabs on my whereabouts, be asked to report my location throughout the day, and my vagina would never get a break.

Whether Chase believes it or not, the forbiddance of our relationship and time apart makes our fuck fest better. Explosive and mind bending. He wants that all of the time. I'm fine with it when I want it. Thanks to Charles.

I change the subject. "I'll go on this sleigh ride, but don't get mad if the helicopter picks us up. I don't take chances in the woods at night."

"I hear you rich lady. Now slide up here and let me bathe you with my tongue."